The dark-haired woman stared at Bishop questioningly.

"Are you—a sort of private detective?" For the first time hostility burned in the green eyes.

"I am not."

The silence extended, was ruffled by a man's sudden laugh at the bar, returned and at last broke:

"Something makes me believe you."

"Good." He was cheerful. "Then I shan't have to convince you."

"You'll have to tell me what you are, though."

"I suppose I shall. Can't quite give it an exact label. I just look for trouble. Other people's. When I find it, I try to help. That's all."

She said nothing. She watched him.

ALSO BY ADAM HALL

Queen in Danger
Bishop in Check
Pawn in Jeopardy
Rook's Gambit

Published by
HarperPaperbacks

ADAM HALL

Knight Sinister

A Hugo Bishop Mystery

HarperPaperbacks

A Division of HarperCollinsPublishers

HarperPaperbacks *A Division of* HarperCollins*Publishers*
10 East 53rd Street, New York, N.Y. 10022

Cover photography by Herman Estevez

First HarperPaperbacks printing: November 1990

Printed in the United States of America

HarperPaperbacks and colophon are trademarks of HarperCollins*Publishers*

10 9 8 7 6 5 4 3 2

For Vivienne and Van
in return for a lost Queen

MOVE

LONDON WAKED.

In Trafalgar Square a flock of pigeons settled in a trembling cloud, down from a dawn-grey sky; and along Oxford Street ran the clangour of milkmen's bottles. Beneath Eros in Piccadilly Circus a man leaned, dead drunk with a picked wallet.

From Victoria a No. 16 bus shouldered out of the red-painted pack and swung away, its conductor whistling, the tune fading among the vomit of exhaust-gas; and from Praed Street in Paddington a black Humber saloon heeled into Edgware Road with its treads yelling over the tarmac and its radio-antennae shivering and its driver snicking into third and clouting the throttle while his orders

1

mouthed metallicly from the 'speaker ... two men
in dark grey Standard coupe number YJD 3034
*making south by Hyde Park calling cab B 17, 19,
21, 23 ... two men in dark grey Standard——*

The black Humber slewed among the early
traffic down towards Marble Arch with its bell frantic for gangway; but the man in Room 302 of the
Ritz did not hear the bell; he was too far away as
he slipped off his blue silk dressing-gown and went
into his shower that was pastel-tiled and agleam
with steamy chromium and glass. On the Embank-
ment another man dragged himself awake, his
limbs aching in outcry against the hard cold bench,
and put his filth-clad feet on to the paving-stones,
and made their soreness bear his shuffling weight
as he walked away with his rags and bones ... the
rags that were his clothing and the bones that were
himself.

In a Hampstead nursing-home a child was born,
three minutes before eight o'clock, and was
brought to breathing life by the confident clinical
hands of the doctor in attendance; and three minutes later, at eight o'clock the black-coated man in
Pentonville pulled the lever, and dropped the
wooden trap, and watched—with the doctor in attendance—the prisoner escape his prison in the
only way offered him ... by means of a hempen
noose. London presented life and death, in a simple
two-act play, while the bottles rattled down Oxford

Street and the buses drummed up Drury Lane and the tugs came down the Thames.

In Streatham a housewife stirred her tea, and a tealeaf rose to the surface while she eyed the clock and looked at her husband, who had ten minutes for his train. A seagull cried above the river, by the wharfs of Wapping Old Stairs, as a body rose to the surface, breaking the scum and staring with a white blind face at the screaming bird.

In Westminster a cleaner tipped a cigar-butt from the ashtray into the bin, and thought of the man who had smoked it, of the man who had once said *I have nothing to offer you but blood, tears, toil, and sweat* . . . and the cleaner remembered the telegram that had told him about his boy. In Charing Cross Road a policeman found a pedlar, and moved him on; in Kensington a small boy finished his corn-flakes, and moved his plate; and in Chelsea a man felt the first sun-shine dream through the window against his back, and moved his hand, and lifted the black Queen diagonally past the Pawn on the chequered board.

As he set the piece down, it was as if this were the key to some kind of combination, for at the far end of the room the door opened, and a woman came in.

"Good morning, Hugo."

For a moment he said nothing but stared at the board with his frown deepening. Then: "Impossible. An utterly im*possible* situation!"

The woman came up to the limed-oak desk, and stood with her arms folded, looking down at the chessmen. Her voice was resigned.

"Well, before you try getting yourself out of it, I want to tell you something. I've found you some work."

His head jerked up and a feather of ash fell from his *meerschaum* pipe to the chessboard.

"Work?"

"Yes. To-day. It might turn out to be dramatic, because it's to do with the stage—"

"I don't want to get mixed up with any fame-bound leading ladies throwing lap-dogs, milk coats, tiaras and temperaments all over the—"

"Shut up."

"Oh." He looked down at the white Queen, which was covered in pipe-ash. "Well what?"

"Well this. It's a young woman named Nicole Pedley. She isn't an actress, but she's in love with an actor. She is also married."

"But not to the actor."

"No, but there's more to it than that."

"There usually is. How old's the baby?"

"There is no baby. All I can tell you just now is that she'll be at the Dutch Inn this evening at six, waiting for you. She has your name. You are someone who might know where to find a man called Trafford. He is the actor she's in love with. He's missing. Will that give you enough lead?"

He got up and traipsed round the room. The sunlight was a warm stream, and trellis-shadow patterned the carpet from the panes. He said:

"Yes. Plenty. I'm very grateful, Gorry."

Miss Gorringe, plump, twice his age, severe in tweeds, turned her colourless eyes on him. Nothing ever showed in them, save the declaration that she would conceal her every thought no matter who looked for them.

"So that's that, Hugo. I've found another mission, like a fool. I wish you'd go and work down a mine or up a steeple. Something safe like that."

He stopped traipsing to look pained.

"Do I ever risk my teeth-skin?"

"With monotony. Look at last month when they put a bomb on your plane—"

"I slung it out, didn't I?"

"What if you hadn't seen it?"

"Then it would've slung me out. I can't be right every time, but I can try." He prodded down the ash in his pipe with a fountain-pen and fumbled for matches. She gave him a box. "Anyway they were a moody gang. This gentle backstage romance you've found for me sounds as risky as whist." Smoke skeined up from the white bowl.

Miss Gorringe shrugged, bending over the chessboard and blowing the ash away from the Queen. "I don't know, it might be dangerous. If it isn't, you'll make it. I'm old enough to be your mother and thank God I'm not; but it's my job to find you these—these missions, and it's like telling a kid to run across a busy street to the sweetshop opposite." She lifted the black Rook, and moved it two squares, straightening up.

Bishop smiled gently. "That's half your fun, working with me, Gorry. You know it might stop, any minute, when I get killed or something comic. Without that feeling of constant climax you'd be bored."

She turned away from the desk, her voice admitting it.

"That's terrible, and quite true. Just don't take any chances, and don't throw any away."

She was not slim; she was fifty and not very tall; but as she walked down the long room to the door she walked with a poise admirable to watch: as she knew he watched, and despite that. The door closed, and for a while he stared at it with a strange mood in his eyes; then he moved and sat again in the black carved chair behind the desk, thinking about the woman who loved the actor who was missing; gazing at the pieces on the chessboard, until at last his thoughts slipped away and the new position of the pieces was registered in his mind.

A smile touched the grey eyes. Miss Gorringe had moved the black Rook two squares, leaving for Hugo Bishop an echo of their conversation. From every side there was now threat. From the Pawn, from the Rook, from the Knight and from the Queen was the threat of instant attack.

In their hostile midst stood the single defenceless piece—the Bishop with the sun's light glaring on the white ivory.

She paid the driver and came through the swing-doors, hurrying until she was inside, as though she didn't want to be seen; then, inside, she slowed her step, glancing round without turning her head. In a corner alcove a man got up, folding a paper. Thin, thirty, light-eyed and with spectacles he now took off and pocketed. His voice was low, a little vague.

"Mrs. Pedley?"

"Yes." Her perfume was tentative, *Haleine de Minuit.* She was slim in bottle-green, deceptively simple, a little *ingenue.* A gold chain winked on her wrist.

"My name's Bishop. Where shall we talk?"

"I—don't know this place."

"All right, how about over here? Got a bar, I think." He went beside her, their shoes silent over pile. "Why choose here, if you don't know it?"

"I didn't. It was you—wasn't it? Your wife said on the phone that you'd be here at six."

"That wasn't my wife. That was Miss Gorringe. Don't laugh, she's an M.A. What'll I bring over?"

"Sherry, please."

"Don't go away."

She thought, as she watched him go to the bar, that he didn't look like a friend of Roy's. Perhaps he wasn't, but just knew where he had gone. She laid her head against the plush, half-closing her green eyes, stopping herself as she thought of Roy, unclenching the small gloved hand.

"Cigarette?" he said, sitting down in the little barrel-chair.

"No thanks."

"Is that the right colour?"

"It looks perfect."

"Your health."

"Yours."

A waiter came past looking worried, very quiet-toned.

"I'm sorry, sir, I didn't see you come in—"

"That's all right, I've coped."

The man went. Bishop murmured, "How is Mr. Pedley?"

The shadow of her lashes fled up to her eyes as they widened. "You know him?"

"No."

The pause lengthened, grew pointed. "He's— very well."

"Yes."

"Harrison Pedley, then. Morton Productions."

"That's right."

8

He wished Gorry could have told him more; he was groping a little. She gave a lead; she had to. Leaning forward with the bangle making a tiny clatter on the table-edge: "I—understand you know where Mr. Trafford has gone." There was fear in her voice, her eyes, that this was wrong.

"You terribly want to see him again, don't you?"

"Isn't that a bit personal?"

"It's a bit obvious. I just wanted to make sure. I'm here to help you, you know. Lend me a hand, would you?"

She found nothing she disliked in the faint, dry smile of his eyes. She had never seen him before, but felt already she knew him well. There was about him an atmosphere of utter, utter calm. You could never panic while he was looking.

"Very well. Yes, I would rather like to see him again."

He meditated with sherry fondling his palate. It was all right now; he had her with him. "Look here, I'm an absolute stranger but I think I can help you a lot. Can I ask a few things first? It'll make it easier."

"You can ask anything, if I can answer only what I like."

"Of course. Please tell me about Trafford. You're in love with him. When did you see him last, and what happened?"

In the green eyes he saw reflected the twin pale

9

images of his own face. The light, shedding from a wall-lamp, lay amber on the smooth line of her throat, gleamed with a warm lustre along the gold links of the necklace. At first uncertainly the lips began moving, hiding and revealing her little teeth.

"We—we last saw each other in his dressing-room at the Olympus. He shared it with another man but he had gone and we—were alone. Roy talked to me while he took off his make-up, then when we were ready to leave he asked me to telephone my husband."

The gold chain winked, its links' reflection winking across the surface of the sherry, honey-brown and gold. A nerve pulsed in her smooth throat. She did not look any more at Bishop.

"That—I think that was how it began. He wanted me to phone Harrison and say I was stopping the night in town, with someone we both knew, a friend, a woman..."

The gold gleamed. The nerve beat. The surface of the sherry was fragile and still. Bishop listened.

"Darling, that would be too dangerous."

"You've done it before. He never objected."

"I know but—it isn't only that; or rather it *is* just that."

He shrugged. "You mean he's so easy to deceive. More fool. When a man cares as little as that about his wife, he deserves—"

"No, Roy. Please understand. To stay with you tonight would be heaven, but—I don't hate him, not as much as to lie and deceive and—"

"You don't love him."

"No, but hate and love are the extremes. There's things in the middle, darling. I respect him; he's a genius in the theatre—"

"Good, anyhow—"

"Very good, yes. He's got a brilliant mind and I'd do anything not to see it hurt. I owe that to him. It might stop him working, might hurt him so deeply that he'd be utterly finished. Please, Roy, see that. How I feel. I'm—torn apart. Don't make it worse."

In the mirror he saw her face, elfin, appealing, defenceless. He looked away from the mirror and held her, moving his chin against her brow, seeing now his own face in the glass and knowing that whatever he asked her she would do, eventually. His voice was vibrant to her; she loved this voice with a strange violence, the face with its dark eyes and firm rebellious mouth.

"I want you to come away with me, Nicole. To marry, after the divorce. I'm going on tour soon— you'll come with me and—"

"You're out of your mind, darling—"

"I love you. Is that madness?"

"Yes, in so many ways." Her breath trembled; her fingers hurt the flesh of his arms as she clung to him. "We could go away but it might do something unthinkable to him; and we should have little money—I know that's trivial but it'd become important when my small funds ran out and—"

"I'm not precisely on the dole."

"Please, oh *please* . . . women are practical, they have to be—"

"So am I. I'm getting ten a week on tour; that won't put us up at the Ritz but . . . besides, I can raise more. Quite a lot. God, isn't it worth it?"

"Worth what, Roy? How would you raise it?" Her hands relaxed, fell away; she buried her face against him. "It doesn't matter anyhow, it isn't only money, it's Harrison."

Quietly he said to his pale face in the mirror, "Yes, I know. I know it's Harrison. But it'll be all right. I'll fix things up, but stay up here to-night . . . please."

She freed herself and leaned against the dressing-table edge, her dark hair fretting with its reflection under the lamp, flecked and shining. Her eyes were wide, and green, and adamant.

"No, Roy. Not if you love me. Another time, some time when I don't have to make up lies and telephone them so deliberately. Much as I want you, it's more than I can do."

He was pale, perhaps after the dark make-up. He spoke very softly, with the voice that might one day establish his name on the stage. But he was not, for this moment, acting.

"All right, darling. We'll leave it at that. I'll see you to the car—if I may?"

Wanting to say she was sorry, to be held again, to thank him for not persisting, something stayed her like a whisper from nowhere, a warning, a reminder, a fear.

"You're—giving in easily to-night, Roy darling."

"Surely you'd prefer that?"

"Oh yes. You—you just seem...strange. Tense."

He lifted a hand to his brow. "I've done two shows to-night and a matinee Wednesday. Bit much."

She was released; the whisper was silenced, fled.

"I'm sorry, dearest. I'm being so beastly. You must be dead-beat." She stroked his hair, smoothing it above the temples, relaxing his tension with tender fingertips. "I'll go now. I won't offer to drop you home, it'll be—too dreadful not to come in. Just know that I want to do that, terribly much my darling."

His mouth smiled; his eyes observed her.

"Give me a ring, Nicole. Any time at all."

The puzzlement returned, fleetingly; she made it go.

"I promise. Soon."

He answered her kiss with less passion than she knew was in him; but he was tired. She slipped from his arms.

"There's grease-paint on your collar again, darling."

13

"Thawpit'll fix that." He was distant, already.

"Yes, I suppose it will." He was tired, and perhaps angry about not ringing Harrison. She couldn't alter that; he mustn't expect her to. "Good night, Roy."

As she left the dressing room she didn't look at him again, knowing what would be in his eyes, the thought of Harrison saying good night to her later, in the same room; fat, brilliant, middle-aged Harrison whose right it was to watch her undressing, the flash of silk across that slim body—while Roy lay in his hotel bedroom alone and with a book, a cigarette.

She closed the door, shutting the scene inside with him, taking her part of it away. Poor, kindly Harrison; poor, frustrated Roy. Where in the world were there people happy, loving without deception, without torment? And what must it be like?

The door of her car clicked shut; she pressed the starter, forgetting she had left it in gear. The starter banged and the car jerked. She would forget other things, if this went on. Things that were safe remembered, dangerous forgotten. Words in her talk with Harrison that might at any moment send her stumbling into even worse than this.

Roy had been so pale, so tense. As if a plan were on his mind, was that quite it? Or perhaps merely tired...two shows to-night and the matinee Wednesday... Tired to death of speaking his lines and thinking between them of the racking circle that ringed the three of them...

———

The gold links winked in the amber light; the two glasses were empty. His lean fingers stuffed the tobacco-shreds into the white *meerschaum* bowl.

The waiter was quick to attend them this time, when Bishop beckoned him. The glasses were replaced; amber rings trembled against the low ceiling like liquid light, reflected upwards.

"And that was two weeks ago."

"Yes."

"Since then?"

"I've telephoned him, two or three times. They said he left his hotel on the Sunday of that week, the day after I said good night to him in the dressing-room. He never went back to the theatre; the A.S.M. had to take over his part for a few nights; now they've an understudy."

"I see. And has he tried to get in touch with you?"

The paper scored a slight dry sound as she took it from her bag. "Yes. He sent a letter."

"Can I read all of it?"

She nodded, passing him the single sheet. Her small face was composed as a mask, only her lips moved. "It's very short," she said.

In a moment he looked up, over the sheet of vellum. His grey eyes were vacant, his voice quite level and expressionless.

"You know that in law they have an ugly name for this."

Her breath was quick, but she did not look away.

"Yes, I know. But—but please don't say it. I don't think it could ever be the truth."

He looked again at the letter. "You want to find him, don't you?" he murmured.

"I do. And can you help?"

He folded the sheet and passed it back to her.

"I think I'd better," he said.

2nd

MOVE

SHE SAID: "I don't quite understand. How do you mean?"

"Because this is a sort of thing that ought not to go on. It ought to be stopped. I'd like you to let me try. You see, from the outsider's viewpoint—my own—one of the two nasty things is happening. Either Trafford is—" he avoided the word—"threatening you that unless you send him more money he'll tell your husband about things; or it isn't true, and he's writing these letters for a different, less obvious reason. In both cases the matter is odd and ugly, and should be got into the daylight. That's as I see it. You're different. The main thing that matters to you is that you find Trafford, so that he can explain, so that you can—take things up where you left off."

She neither admitted nor denied the implication. She had listened with her small gazelle's head slightly on one side, attentively, and now voiced her surprise.

"I've just realized that fifteen minutes ago I had never seen you; and now we're discussing my rather cheap affair and . . . this letter. Is it that I've been longing to tell someone—anyone? Preferably a stranger whose opinion can't matter to me?"

"Partly that. Partly because I've played you a dirty trick."

"I wondered, yes." Her expression did not change. "You don't know where Roy Trafford is. Do you?

"How did we meet here, then? A friend of mine said that someone called Bishop might help. So I rang your number."

"Believing that 'might help' meant 'might know where Trafford is.'"

"Of course. What else?" She left her lips parted a little, and he heard the soft intake of breath. "Are you—a sort of private detective?" For the first time hostility burned in the green eyes.

"I am not."

The silence extended, was ruffled by a man's sudden laugh at the bar, returned and at last broke:

"Something makes me believe you."

"Good." He was cheerful. "Then I shan't have to convince you."

"You'll have to tell me what you are, though."

"I suppose I shall. Can't quite give it an exact label. I just look for trouble. Other people's. When I find it, I try to help. That's all."

"I see. Just a gay cavalier. The world's best friend. And what's your fee?"

"This is where I excuse myself and retire, but I'm not going to, even after that." He held his sherry-glass an inch off the table, watching through its transparency the blood recede from the pad of his fingers as he pressed it against the outside. His print was etched, whitely against the glass. He found the right words. "You'll have to trust your intuition, Mrs. Pedley. In helping people who've got a lot on their minds, I learn about them, I learn a great deal. It's rather fascinating—and please don't bring in guinea-pigs—and one day I'm going to analyse the whole gamut, in a book. I haven't thought of a title yet. Probably something pompous, like 'Personality under Stress'. But you know what I mean."

She said nothing. She watched him. He looked up, and smiled gently.

"Am I the first Colorado Beetle you've ever seen?"

After a bit she said softly, "I wonder how big a fool I'm being. You have a kind of weird spell."

"My grandmother was a goblin. Does that help?" Her smile was hesitant.

"A little, perhaps. This friend of mine, who said a man named Bishop might help—she was Moira Black. You know her?"

"No."

"Then she knows you. Or of you."

"Possibly. Lots of people know me. Some of them think I'm quite nice."

"I can ask her, you know."

"I'll save you the trouble. She'll say that Betty What's-it mentioned my name, because she'd heard it from Tony Whoever, and *he* got it from— oh, maybe half a dozen people. But in the end you'll come to a very dear friend of *mine*. Miss Vera Gorringe, M.A. The lady you telephoned when you looked for Bishop in the directory."

She watched him with a feline gaze, perhaps with a certain relief in pursuing a new problem, different from the one that had sent her here to this strange person. When he had finished she said:

"Now I should like a cigarette."

He lit it for her, breaking the match accidentally as he struck it.

"Sorry."

"It doesn't matter. For you, that was incredibly clumsy."

"I take that as a compliment."

"You may."

The smoke lifted. "Thank you for explaining, Mr. Bishop. Do you still want to help me?"

"Only if you trust me completely; and there's no reason why you should."

"There isn't, but I shall. I don't quite know why. Intuitively, perhaps."

"Good." He stared for a moment at the broken match-end in the tray; then his tone changed and lost its faint amusement. "This was the first letter you had from Trafford. When did it come?"

"A week ago. Last Saturday."

"You replied?"

"Yes."

"To the address here?"

"Yes."

"Sent money?"

"I—yes, I did. Perhaps I—"

"Shouldn't have, quite . . . however. Was your letter acknowledged?"

"Yes, on Wednesday."

"Was it a cheque you sent, or notes?"

"A cheque."

"We can soon trace that."

She let out a little pent breath. She hated telling anyone this, but—"It was signed by Harrison. It was his cheque. I—I was low in funds. Two hundred is a lot of money."

Bishop nodded, tampering thoughtfully with his pipe. She added: "You must think I'm a perfect

21

bitch, taking it from my husband to pay my lover. Why am I talking to you like this, so frankly?"

"If you weren't you'd be busting by now. You had to tell someone. No, I don't think you're a bitch at all. You don't mind whether Trafford is paid the money or not; he isn't destitute. But you mind very much that he doesn't go to Harrison with the story. That's what you're paying for, or what Harrison is. It might prove fair value. Your husband would give a lot more than that to believe you and he are still all right. That's a cockeyed view but it must suffice for now. Have you been to his address?"

"No."

"No?"

She met his frank gaze defensively, said nothing. He puckered a lip. "Afraid you won't find him there: or will, and find he's no explanation for you?"

The words grated across a small dry tongue: "Something like that."

"Does the address mean anything to you? Is it one of Trafford's friends?"

"I don't know. I've never heard it before."

"All right. When you decide to trust me by telling the truth, you know my number." He was standing up, taking his gloves from the table. He heard her choke softly on a breath, saw the deep green eyes widen as she stared at him. Then, as she sat quite without movement, her small hands on her lap and her dark head tilted, the deep green eyes grew swiftly lustrous and a glint moved down, a tear across her cheek. It fell so strangely like a raindrop from a clear sky.

"That was silly of me," she said. Her tone was rough, dry, velvet; a little harsh and over-controlled. "Do I have another chance?"

He leaned over her, touching her elbow gently.

"It's gloomy in here. Outside there's sun. Coming?"

It flooded them, brazen and golden, as they went through the swing-doors. He knew how rotten she must be feeling because she hadn't even asked for time off to go and fix her mascara in the cloakroom. Along the sparkling pavement he said, "Would you be seen dead in this?"

Vaguely she stopped, looking at the Rolls-Royce. It was immaculate, the cellulose had a showroom finish; the plating was impeccable; but the car sat high on the road and its lines were vintage.

"It's magnificent," she smiled. He opened the door.

"Venerable, maybe. Born in 1920; a gallant old girl."

The surge of acceleration was silken and subdued; he swung left and parked again, just off the Mall.

"It'd be nice to go for a ride, but time's short and we ought to talk. All right?"

She nodded. She had busied with a mirror and things.

"Good. Why didn't you want to tell me about this address?"

"I—I'm not certain." She moved half round in the seat, half facing him, leaning her head against the glass of the window. "Please believe that. It's just that—I got the shivers, when I went. It was so queer. So odd."

He waited, a little impatiently. "Yes?"

"Perhaps, when I've told you, you might see what I mean. It was almost perfectly ordinary, yet there was something...the address is a florist's in South Kensington. A small shop, flowers, seeds, bulbs."

The sunshine, slanting down through the windscreen with a westering mellow warmth, touched her hair tawnily, flecked it with bronze glints. In the intimacy of the car her voice was soft and slow.

"A small man, too, in the shop. Quite old and very wrinkled, and so sweet. A sort of gentleman-gnome, like the coloured earthenware one that stood in a dark corner. He called me Madam, with much courtesy."

The sun dreamed in her hair, finding a pleasure there in the colouring it made. Her voice breathed quietly in the car.

"I beg pardon, Madam—a Mr.—?"

"Trafford. Mr. R. Trafford."

His eyebrows, grey and bushy and questioning,

lifted; the brow, parchment-pale and with thin blue veins, furrowed anew.

"I'm sorry, Madam—so very sorry." His narrow head wagged gently like a disappointed bird's. "Did he make a purchase here . . . perhaps?"

The scent of wallflowers came sweetly from the shadows of the shop. From a beam, herbs hung down in an enormous and shaggy bunch, drying, punctuating the scent with an acrid care.

"I don't think so. I—received a letter from him this address. This is Sixteen, Tallow Lane?"

His perplexity increased. "Why, yes, that is correct, Madam. But—"

"Are there flats, above?"

"Only my own, and a floor where there are things in store. Perhaps the handwriting—would it be Fifteen, or Ten—"

"It was typewritten."

The wallflowers had a sickly smell; their scent had become a cloying breath in the small warm shop. The herbs hung down, shaggy and matted like the dead hair of a man, his feet trussed at the beam.

From a dark corner a gnome grinned with bright red cheeks and a bright red nose and painted sightless eyes. His head was tilted.

"Then there has been some mistake, Madam." The head of the old man was tilted, too, in apology. "However, if a Mr. Trafford calls here at any time,

I should be very happy to acquaint you if you would care to leave your address."

His eyes were hopeful that such a chance might come of assisting the lady, his shoulders a little hunched beneath the problem that neither could for the moment solve, his pale, thin-veined hands spread to emphasise his humble offer.

"I—that's very kind of you, but—it doesn't matter, thank you." She felt stifled and the rich redolence from the shadows bespelled her senses with an evil subtlety; the shaggy head hung upside down and screamed without a sound. She turned, jerkily, to go, as if shaking off the influence of a drug—

"Oh, Madam..."

Her breath caught as she turned back at the doorway.

"Yes?"

Even the sun, slanting across one of her shoulders, had a strange effect upon her senses. In contrast with its warm bright benison the shadows and the perfume and the darkling gnome crowded in the shop, holding her back from the ordinary street where buses went.

"Madam—" his pale hand fluttered to a shelf— "I wonder perhaps if you would accept this little packet?" He was offering it deferentially, slightly bowing, almost hesitant. She looked down at the packet of seeds, with its design of rioting colour— aubretia among mellow stones.

"They are a sample," he said, smiling. "For your rockery."

The words reached her through a cloud of doubts and eldritch fancies. "Rockery?"

He inclined his head. She said:

"You know I have a rockery?"

"Aubretia grows anywhere, Madam."

Suddenly she was walking along the sunlit pavement, faster and faster until the chill faded from her spine and the sky lifted above her head, blue and familiar, and the buses slid squarely past her, red and familiar, and a ragged man offered her matches from his gutter-tray, so that she bought a box for a shilling because that, too, was familiar. She was home again, from a strange place she had fled without knowing why.

She opened her bag and put the match-box in, next to the packet of seeds.

3rd

MOVE

"THAT SOUNDS QUITE ORDINARY."

She smiled, a little ashamed.

"Yes, doesn't it? But I haven't embroidered. The sensation was very real, and quite frightening."

He started the engine and it idled, a stream of soft percussion, while he gazed up the street against the sunshine. "If the old boy had said yes, he knew Mr. Trafford, I think the wallflowers would have smelt just like wallflowers, and the gnome would've been made of earthenware. It would have been what you expected: the address was right—you were sure you'd find Trafford, or hear word of him. You met the unexpected, the denial. Already upset, you felt worse than ever, more at a loss. Don't you think?"

She nodded.

"Perhaps."

The gear grated slightly. As they swung into the traffic-flow he said: "Where shall I drop you?"

"Anywhere."

"Going home?"

"I think I will, now."

"Very far?"

"Hampstead."

He turned into Jermyn Street and went across the Circus into Charing Cross Road. "I'll try to find Trafford," he said. "Can't guarantee anything. Just carry on as though we'd never met, will you? If he writes, write back."

"Very well. What if anything happens? Shall I phone you?"

"Please. If I'm not there, you can tell Miss Gorringe anything you could tell me. It's awfully important that you rely on that."

"I'll remember. Will you go to the little shop?"

"I shall go to a lot of odd places."

They slid by a bus along Tottenham Court Road and heard the Special Edition yell from the boys outside Warren Street tube.

Later he said, "Shall I take you right to the gates?"

"I don't think it matters."

The surge of the cylinders died away.

"You're feeling a bit done-up, aren't you?"

"A bit." There was little tension in her face, but the smile was tired. "I started the day by thinking

I was going to meet someone who knew where Roy was. Sorry if I look like a pricked balloon." Her stockings flashed in the deepening sun's rays as she slipped from the seat and gave the door a little slam.

"My fault," he said. "I'll try to make up for it."

Her hand was very small in his, the wrist slightly arched with a dark brown mole just above the gold bangle.

"You have," she murmured. "I don't know why, but I feel a lot more cheerful than I should. I suppose that's contradictory."

"Whatever it is, stay in the mood. Good-bye."

The sun flashed once across the screen like a fierce blood-swab as he turned; then it was behind, poised above the Heath. Her slim figure was still for a moment by the gates; a small maroon-red glove was lifted; then the exhaust's whisper faded, and the air was calm, and a bird called and then sped from a bough like a flung dart.

"Who lef' this blinkin' ol' Rolls 'ere?"

"I dunno."

"Out o' the Ark, eh? Whose is it?"

"I dunno."

"Well, 'ow can other people get in an' out?"

"That's your 'eadache."

"Good mind to push it along the Museum."

"Want somethin' to do, don't you?"

"Well fancy leavin' it 'ere?"

"Yers. Fancy."

The thin man with big ears sidled away. It was time he swept the steps down. The other man raised his eyebrows at the ancient object of his displeasure, and went back to the cool shadow of the stage door. The car wasn't in anyone's way. He just felt like that. He always felt like this of a morning, especially when the sun was out. Wanted to move everything he could lay hands on. Rolls-Royce, fruit-barrows, whole of Shaftesbury Avenue. Set the world right, that was Tom.

He picked up a broom and went down the long stone passage, and stopped, and thought better of it, and came back and put the broom in his office. Then he went down the passage without it and through the double doors. The boards were littered with cabling, props, boxes and Chippies' tools.

He stood, thoughtful, with his hands in his pockets, getting an oblique view through the wings.

"Ah, balmy breath, that dost almost persuade Justice to break her sword! One more, one more. Be thus when thou art dead, and I will kill thee. And love thee after. One more, and this the last—"

"Can you lean back even more, Mathieson?"

"All right."

"As long as the light's across the upper part of her face—"

"Shall I shift the spot over, sir? Just an inch?"

"Could try."

"Be thus when thou art dead, and I—"

"Just a minute...Todd, don't bring it too low."

"Right, sir."

"Try it there. Thank you, Matt."

In the wings Dincock murmured, "He must imagine he's on a bloody film-set."

"He knows what he's doing. Look at it last week and look at it now."

"He's overdoing it. We'll be so keen on positioning everyone'll dry."

"You'll dry whatever happens, ol' boy."

"Who's there? Othello?"

"I! Desdemona."

"Will you come to bed, my lord?"

"Have you prayed to-night, Desdemona?"

"Ay, my lord."

"More surprise, Marion—puzzlement..."

"Ay, my lord."

"Better, yes. Try a rising inflection; begin low—almost a question."

"Ay...my lord—?"

Dincock said: "My God, he's going to run us into the early hours at this rate."

"We can always sleep in the stalls. That's Harrison all over."

"Oh, it'll be worth it. He's all right."

"Make up your mind..."

> *"Talk you of killing?"*
> *"Ay, I do."*
> *"Then heaven have mercy on me!"*
> *"Amen, with all my heart!"*

The round balding head moved among the rows of plush.

"Wring that right out, would you...you really mean that, remember."

> *"Amen...with all—my—heart!"*

The round head nodded. The soft brown eyes watched, while the mind ranged over the mood of the lines and saw, instead of Mathieson's tweed suit and pallid features, the black beard and the great jewelled scabbard, the thin bright flames of the candles in the sconce...

"...No, by my life and soul!"
Send for the man, and ask him!
"Sweet soul, take heed,
"Take heed of perjury; thou art on thy death-bed."

... The candles, burning pale and fearful in their sconce ... the white, bewildered face, the widening eyes awakened to the relentless mood of the Moor whose jealousy craved death and nothing less for its placation ...

> *"Down, strumpet!"*
> *"Kill me to-morrow: let me live to-night!"*
> *"Nay, if you strive—"*
> *"—But half an hour!"*
> *"Being done, there is no pause...."*
> *"But while I say one prayer!"*
> *"...It is too late."*

Pedley's head was lowered a little and his eyes watched with an attention that froze his features into a plump, clean-shaven mask. On the stage the woman gasped and Mathieson's body trembled, arched above her, his hands about the white throat. Pedley said: "Good!" and his head lifted. The mask relaxed; the eyes calmed; he turned to Nicole in the seat beside him and whispered something.

She nodded, unable to return his brief smile.

"They're good, Harrison, yes."

He patted her hand quickly and went up on to the stage; in a moment he was the centre of three or four people: the actors, a carpenter, the chief electrician. They gestured; Pedley spoke; someone nodded; the electrician pointed to the wings; and Nicole watched the miming and pressed her crossed knee against the seat-back in the next row, the words brittle in her mind, sniggering maliciously in her mind...*Down, strumpet!...kill me to-morrow: let me live to-night!...it is too late*...

In the wings Dincock went over his lines, not speaking aloud but drumming the words against the palate with the tongue. Beside him, Ferson lit a half-cigarette that he had doused earlier on his due. Behind them, Tom the stage-door-keeper shuffled off to find something he could do to set the world right. There was nothing for him here. Mr. Pedley'd got the monopoly.

The voices droned, ebbing in sharp waves into the open wastes of the auditorium. In the gallery two cleaners took up their gear again. A carpenter began hammering somewhere.

"...See if we can get a bigger sconce—four candles. Then Todd can go to town with his spot..."

"...Didn't hurt you, did I?"

"Only a bit—"

"Terribly sorry, darling, a spring or something gave way on the damned bed and I had to lean on your throat—"

"Use my stomach next time, it's more robust..."

"...Then we can have more light thrown—lots of reflection on this side—take long to paint, Williams?"

"Half-hour, sir, rough. Finish it later..."

Ferson smoked, leaning one shoulder against a

post. Dincock larynxed his lines. Mrs. Pedley sat very still, six rows back, and watched the producer, wondering if he were capable ... if he would obey an impulse ... or, like the outraged Moor, deliberately ... *Down, strumpet! ... it is too late ... too late ...*

She lit a cigarette, quickly, and looked away from the producer, and saw the call-boy sitting on a crate munching an apple, and Ferson, smoking in the wings. The carpenter hammered, the sound choking harshly into the auditorium to the gallery, the circle, the high shadows where Hugo Bishop sat, watching quite alone.

The hammering stilled; Pedley's voice came loudly; the call-boy jerked upright on the crate and for a moment his munching stopped. Nicole looked back at the producer, admiring the command with which he moved the others as a player would move the pieces across a chequerboard. Would he, one day ... one night ... sacrifice his Queen?

If Roy told him, for any reason told him, what would Harrison do? Harrison, kind, tolerant, too filled with the wonder of his work, too confident of her love for him ... in such a mind, might not something snap?

"Same again, then. Try it both ways, Todd, and see how we shape. All right, Mathieson?"

"Hell," Dincock muttered in the wings, "I'm going out for a beer."

"You'll get flayed if you're wanted."

"Colonel Bogey to that."

He went off, one of his corduroy turn-ups flicking the dusty boards.

In the shadows of the circle, Bishop left his seat and vanished soundlessly. Pedley came down left, nodding.

"All right," he said.

"Be thus when thou art dead, and I will kill thee,
And love thee after . . . One more, and this the
  last."

The words lifted, eddied, drifted outwards across the empty seats, reaching the farthest walls and there falling in soft cadences, like leaves dying down the wind.

"Did you ring Freddie?"

"I did. The hotel notified them on the Monday evening. Since then he's been officially missing."

"Did you talk to the hotel?"

"Yes, to the manager himself. He said they didn't worry about Trafford until the evening, thinking he might have stayed somewhere unexpectedly on Sunday night. When he didn't come in by seven on Monday evening, they rang the Olympus. He hadn't shown up there either, so they got on to the police."

Bishop filled his pipe vaguely, and small shreds

of tobacco fell to the carpet. Miss Gorringe watched them with an idle interest. He said:

"Formally? Or had he left a lot of bills unpaid?"

"They didn't seem anxious about him."

"M'm. We can assume then that though there's the possibility of his being found in a river or under a bus, the fact that his hotel-bill is paid up to date makes the matter less upsetting. Did Freddie send a man round?"

"I imagine so. It's routine."

The last shred fell; he struck a match, and for a moment the ample Miss Gorringe disappeared, to hover indistinctly like a smoke-screened ship.

"What else?" he said at last.

She took up the newspaper from his desk, and with both hands brought it down sharply through the air. The smoke swirled away, dispersing.

"Oh, *there* you are," she murmured. "Well, there's this else."

He looked at the item she pointed out.

"Dated the twenty-first," she added.

"Ye-es. Exactly a week after Mrs. Pedley saw him last, at the theatre. I somehow doubt if it's anything to do with 'loss of memory', though. Loss of something, but not that."

"Life?" Her large colourless eyes were fixed on him.

He shrugged.

"Too early to say." He dropped the paper to the

desk, and struck another match. "There's a smell of death about it, Gorry; but not necessarily his." The match-stalk pinged into the metal tray. "And it may not have happened yet."

Vera Gorringe got some scissors, cut out a few lines from the paper, and filed the cutting in a spring-back folder. "Are you thinking of Mrs. Pedley, Hugo?"

"Perhaps. I know *she* is. The poor child's frightened."

"She say?"

"No. You could just feel it when you went near her." He told her about Trafford, the letter of blackmail, Mrs. Pedley's reply, Harrison Pedley's cheque. "She went to the address; it was a florist's. An old man said he'd never heard of Trafford. For some reason she got the heebie-jeebies and almost ran out of the shop."

Miss Gorringe's face, aged but with perfect make-up, softened as she slid the spring-back into place on its shelf. "The poor little wretch must be living in a nightmare," she said quietly. "If she believes there's a risk of Trafford's telling her husband—"

"Exactly, or a risk of his finding out, even if Trafford says nothing. I went into the Parthenon this morning and watched Pedley producing *Othello*."

She swung her head to look at him.

"Oh, my Lord . . . and was she there too?"

"Yes."

"Just sitting fascinated, working herself up into an orgy of morbid imagination?"

He nodded, saying crisply: "Yes."

Miss Gorringe pursed her lips, prodding with light fingers at her blue-tinted *coiffure*, a little at a loss.

"Hugo, we'll have to be so careful. Can't she go away for a week? In a week you'll have cleared the whole thing up, and—"

"Think so?"

"You don't know your speed. But she ought to get away from Pedley, until you've sorted things out for her. Pedley's probably the last person in the world to lose enough of his reason to be violent or revengeful, and if Trafford really talked, or Pedley just found out, nothing would happen; nothing like that. But she isn't so sure."

Her hands were restless; the sunlight sparked across a brilliant on her finger. She finished lamely, "I'm—a bit sorry for Mrs. Pedley."

Bishop was watching her through half-closed lids, the smoke climbing in a soft blue vine from the white bowl.

"You've a deeper sense of real pity than any other person I know, Gorry."

She moved quickly, looking out of the window.

"Don't start fitting me for haloes, for Pete's sake. I'm just sorry for the kid, that's all. Isn't that quite natural?"

"No. You ought to say she's a painted Jezebel and should be made to wear a big scarlet letter A—"

"Don't be comic, Hugo. Women don't cuckold their husbands deliberately. The act is deliberate, but the necessity is not. That simply happens, and usually the wife has a worse time than the poor insulted husband. If you can persuade her to take a week off from driving herself into a fever, I should do it. She must have plenty of friends she can stay with."

"I'll see how things go."

He crossed the room and picked up his gloves and ash stick. Her voice floated down the distance to the door.

"You said you can smell death about this case. Not likely to be yours, is it?"

"See no reason, but if I feel a throat coming on, I'll gargle. Back soon."

He went out. King's Road was clogged with traffic, flamboyant with flowers whose brightness bloomed from the barrows where men stood, brown-armed in collarless shirts, shouting in the sunshine. A woman dropped a French loaf and Bishop picked it up for her; she thanked him and walked away, vivid orange bolero and dark green corduroys, small flat sandals and lynx-gait . . . a bad artist, a good rent-ower, but at least another patch of colour in the street where it was all.

The shop was shady, and for a moment Bishop

blinked his eyes, putting his glasses on and folding the letter so that only two lines showed, unintelligibly.

"Hello, Jim."

"Morning, Mr. Bishop."

"Give this type a name for me, would you?"

The man looked at the two lines and then switched on a counter lamp. "Do what I can, sir. It's not anything very standard." He fished behind a cabinet and brought back a thick book with a tattered cover, thumbing through curling pages, laying the letter against two or three of them before he looked up.

"Got it?" Bishop said.

"That's right. Steinrohl Portable, Mark IV. Say about 1935." He passed back the letter.

"Thanks. How's the wife?"

"Oh, middling now. Cussin' a bit through having to stay in bed, but we'll have her up in a week."

Bishop laid the bunch of gladioli on the counter, gently.

"Tell her from a distant admirer," he said.

Jim Proctor put his head on one side, and smiled.

"She'll know who they're from, Mr. Bishop. They're wonderful, aren't they..."

"Good enough to throw at your head when she gets really bored with sitting in bed all day. Tell her I think she's a lazy good-for-nothing."

"I'll say that."

"So-long, Jim."

The sunlight deluged down again as he reached the pavement, impressing on his memory the name of the typewriter until it was etched. Then he stopped a cab.

"Sadler's Hotel."

"Where's that?" the man asked.

"Somewhere behind the Oratory."

"I know. Arches Street."

They set off. When they reached the four-storey building Bishop went in. The assistant manager was a pleasant woman with a vast corsage.

"No, it's stored for him. We had to let his room, but it's all packed when he—if he—I suppose you don't know where he's gone?"

"I'm afraid not, but I'm trying to find out. You might be able to help me: is there a typewriter among his things?"

"I believe so."

"May I see it?"

"Well . . . er—" She fluttered with hesitation.

"I quite understand. All I want really is the name of the machine. Would that be possible?"

"Oh, I think so."

She asked him to wait, and came back within a minute.

"It's an 'Imperial'. Is that helpful?"

"It might be. A portable model, I imagine?"

"Oh, yes, quite compact, with a case."

"Thanks. I appreciate that."

She came to the doors with him: "Do you think Mr. Trafford will be back soon, or has something—awful—happened?" Her eyes gleamed behind their glasses, expecting perhaps a *little* dramatic information when there were such possibilities.

"I don't think anything's happened at all," Bishop said vaguely. "Friend of mine asked me to look up the man, and I'm trying to locate him. Good day."

"Oh. Er—good-bye."

Bishop walked into Old Brompton Road, looked at a windowful of very expensive pipes and tobacco-bowls, and after a while came to Tallow Lane. The strange thing was that his interview with the little old man followed almost exactly the same lines as Mrs. Pedley's.

He used, as far as he could remember accurately, the same questions: he had received a letter from Mr. Trafford bearing this address; the letter was typed and there was no mistaking the number or the street; he was most puzzled to find that the number was not known here.

He received, as far as he could remember accurately, the same answers: Mr. Trafford was *not* known here; there were two floors above the shop, the one accommodating his flat, the other store-rooms; so that there must be some mistake. He was very, and courteously, sorry.

The other odd thing was that Bishop was offered

no sample seeds for his rockery. He felt quite ne-
glected about this, and walked from Knightsbridge
through St. James's Park, going down Whitehall
thinking a lot about the flower shop and poking at
stray cigarette-packets and bus-tickets with his
ash-plant.

When he reached Inspector Frisnay's office he
was let in without much fuss, and this was molli-
fying after his failure to receive free packets of
seeds.

"Hello, cock," Frisnay said. Then he went on
writing.

"Still a common boy," Bishop said, and sat down
after removing the Inspector's shoes from the only
vacant chair. "Soled and heeled, Freddie?"

"What?"

"Doesn't matter. You busy?"

Frisnay put his pen down and lit a cigarette. He
had known Bishop long enough to know that a cigarette wouldn't interest him.

"Of course I'm busy. Now pick my brains and get
it over with."

He was a lean man with hair that wouldn't stick
down and good level eyes. When he moved his eyes
he did it quickly and with a very slight jerk of his
head, so that one had the impression of an instant
and rigid scrutiny. He did this even when he looked
at the time or a stray dog, so it didn't reveal anything dramatic like a razor-keen mind. Other

things did; they were less discernible.

"Gorry phoned you," said Bishop.

"About Trafford. Well?"

Bishop stroked the smooth white bowl of his pipe, looking down at the ash inside, seeing the mass of herbs that had hung from the ceiling of the little shop.

"Someone's had a letter, written by Trafford. They got it last Saturday, week ago to-day. The address—"

"Half a mo'. We had a call from his hotel on the Monday before that. Right?"

"Yes."

"All right. Just want to get the dates straight. Sergeant Flack's the man you want to see, so you can think yourself lucky I know what the hell you're talking about. Go on."

"The address on the letter was Sixteen, Tallow Lane. It's a florist's shop. The person who got the letter went along there, but they said they didn't know Trafford from Tolstoy and they didn't know why he should use that address. They said there was some mistake, which is a nice way of calling someone a bloody liar."

Frisnay stretched out a thin hand and collected a telephone. Bishop said, "When X called at the shop, X was given a free packet of seeds on leaving."

"Flack...." He nestled his temple against the

phone and added, "Go on."

"To-day," Bishop said carefully, "I went to the shop myself. I asked precisely the same question—did they know Trafford? They—"

"Flack? Anything come in on Trafford, missing a fortnight?" Bishop waited.

Frisnay cradled the phone. "Not a sausage," he grunted. "Well?"

"They gave me exactly the same answers as X got."

"Don't keep calling her X—let's call her Fifi or something human."

Bishop looked pained.

"Did I say it was a woman?"

"Yes. Or you could have used 'he' and 'him'."

"What an astute policeman!"

"You flatter yourself. What you mean is that it was natural enough for the shop to say it hadn't heard of Trafford, but it was odd that it didn't tell *you* that yours was the second puzzling enquiry. And it didn't tell you that?"

"No. My enquiry had all the appearance of the first of its kind, according to the answers I got."

Frisnay nibbled his cigarette contemplatively.

"I agree it's queer. If it had been genuine, the man—it was a man in the shop and not another X?—would have said: 'That's funny—a lady was here making the same enquiry!' What else struck you?"

"I wasn't given a free packet of seeds."

Frisnay eyed him with his flicking look and said, after a moment, "Of course if you go about looking for downright charity—"

Bishop cut in. "Stop clowning, Freddie. Surely you can see this is something strong? You may not imagine a missing small-part actor makes much odds, but I think you'll find it does. There's something going on backstage."

"Such as?"

Bishop spread his hands palm downwards and fingers wide. "Listen. Trafford went off without a word to his hotel or to his theatre. The only sign of him since is a letter—sent six days later and postmarked South Kensington and bearing a Tallow Lane address—which was typed, as apparently most of his letters were typed, but not on his own machine, which is still at the hotel. I go to the Tallow Lane address, and the man there keeps strictly mum about the lady who called before me. Now he was *puzzled* when *she* called—or appeared to be. When *I* called, he should have been *damned* puzzled—*if* he really didn't know Trafford's name."

"All right, so he does know, and he's keeping mum. Actor has to do a quick bunk—probably owes a money-lender or a month's rent—and with his last quids fixes a shopkeeper to let him use an accommodation address with no questions answered. My dear Bishop, we've enough trouble finding people who are missing by accident, without wasting our time on debt-riddled bunkers."

Bishop looked impatient.

He said, "But Trafford's dead."

Frisnay lifted his head slowly, and didn't say anything for a moment. Then, "That a guess?"

"Not entirely."

"Going to give me any more?"

"Not now. Later, perhaps."

"If anyone but you came in here and told me a man we're looking for is dead, I'd either keep him here until he'd told me everything or I'd say go and make wild guesses somewhere else. Now why do I treat you differently?"

"Because it pays. Always has." Bishop got up. "I just thought that, out of pure benevolence to my old Sixth-Form bully, I ought to drift along and suggest you tell Sergeant Flack to stop thinking of Trafford as merely missing and start thinking of graves."

Frisnay hunched himself higher in his chair and said, "Stay for a cup o' tea while you're here."

"Said the spider to the fly." Bishop reached the door. "You can pick your own brains now, sonny. And when you've put a good man on watching number Sixteen, Tallow Lane, and he's got you some nice dope on who goes in and out, you might remember your little Sixth-Form victim of ancient times, and pass it on. Otherwise he won't stroll in

here and do your job for you when he's feeling kind.
Ta-ta."

Frisnay looked at the panels of his door and
picked up a telephone.

"Flack..." he said.

4th

MOVE

HE WORE A FLOPPY PANAMA, yellowed by summers; it left only the jutting chin unshadowed and accentuated the roundness of his face. He looked a little like Mussolini, except for his eyes; they alone windowed an intelligence and a sensitivity that seemed out of place in the round, placid face.

From the beds, roses came against her closed eyes in warm cadences as the breeze stirred; their scent brought their colour, and she did not have to look. The sun burned on her bare legs, her throat, her arms, lulling and blinding even against the closed lids. The letter was read in her mind, again and again in her mind.

A slight sound hummed bemusedly among the roses.

"Where the bee sucks..." Pedley murmured.

"Mustn't quote," she said. "You're meant to be resting." It was a light retort; she had made it with an effort that was almost frightening, for she was a bad pretender. She sat here, stretched on the extending deck-chair, pretending to love the sunshine, the scents and the sounds of the garden; just as she had pretended to enjoy the lunch that Maria had cooked so well. They lazed, on this Saturday afternoon, the producer and the actress; the one brilliant and professional, the other amateur, and bad, and a little desperate that her lines were right.

"How d'you think it's shaping?" he asked.

"Very well, Harrison. Very firmly."

They were all right, at least; those lines had been rehearsed, and said before of other plays. Harrison asked for reassurance and never flattery. Had she said the new Othello was shaping brilliantly he would never have grunted, and begun to pick holes in his work; because he would know there was not yet brilliance in it. It was simple slogging, until the first night; only then would be seen what measure of brilliance it possessed above older productions. He knew it was shaping well, and firmly. To tell him anything else would dissatisfy him.

He said, "Yes, I think so. I think we'll be all right."

She envied him, and with a sudden vicious

anger that forced her lids apart and focused her eyes, pupils pinpointed against the glare to view his slack fleshy figure in its tennis-shirt and ducks. She envied him, with a senseless passion that slowly cooled, his sole and simple problem—the production of his play. Poor Harrison, lying sun-enwrapped in his fool's paradise...

"Helen came in to see me yesterday," he said. His soft brown eyes watched a starling, its iridescent feathers spangled against a red-brick chimney.

"Helen who?" Nicole asked.

The letter—the second letter—had been here by the second post, waiting for her when they came home for lunch. Yesterday, when she had talked to the strange Mr. Bishop, there had been only one; now there were two. He had said: if he writes, write back. She would, to-day; but she would not enclose another cheque. It was too soon on top of the other. She must see him, now.

"Helen Ledine." His rich tones murmured from his inert frame; the starling darted from the chimney and dipped away over the rockery and down towards the kitchen-garden. "She's rather a dear, but of course I'd nothing for her."

"I don't like her," Nicole said. She hated the way his neck bulged between the collar of his shirt and the panama brim. Yet he was a gentle man, a brilliant man; his fee for such a mind was paid by his physique. "Surely she wasn't thinking of Othello?"

"Partly—understudy, you know. And wanted to know what I was doing next."

"She has a nerve."

He smiled, turning to look at her, squinting in the strong warm light. "Why don't you like her?"

"Oh, no actual reason. She's just one of the many ageing vamps who grow more and more desperate as they see it coming."

"Now, if you were on the stage, my girl, I'd murmur 'sour grapes'. Helen's all right. She won't quit for years; but I admit Shakespeare's got nothing for her."

"Maugham, perhaps."

The smile puckered his fleshy mouth more deeply; he closed his eyes. "Well somebody's got to play in Maugham. And as she's just the type— slinky figure and plenty of animal fire—I sent her along to Tony."

Nicole made another effort, and listened to her voice. It had just the right inflection.

"Portrait of producer passing the buck..."

"If we must be vulgar."

"Better then being pompous."

"*Touché*. But you say I must rest, and proceed to flay quite a decent little actress under my nose. I've little doubt it's pure unbridled jealousy."

"It probably is."

His plump hands folded across his stomach, and

she was startled to think that he might really believe that. With this slight, ironic shock she had a sudden swamping of pity for his utter defencelessness. With a word she could pierce his confidence, conceit...and with a little pin, bore through his castle wall...but she sat in silence with a mother's pity for the slack and gifted man who would never hear the word, unless it came from someone else.

From Roy? Not if she could see him first, ask him to explain the letters, the absence, the incredible change. In a little while she would write; just the four brief words. He would get them on Monday if they were sent to-morrow or to-night. He would collect them from the gentle, hideous old man in the strange dark shop, and would probably be told that she had called there.

Did Roy go there himself, or were her letters merely sent on? Her eyes closed slowly, and the bulging neck and the yellowed straw hat were blotted out by her blood-red lids. Instead there was the lean shadowy strength of the younger face, the vital ardour of the longer eyes, the chiseled flare of nostrils and the black hair that drew upwards from the brow like a wing curved against his head.

His voice would be quiet in the small dark shop; he would stand with his long legs a little astride as he spoke to the man. Roy would visit, burningly alive, the place where her nervous ghost had fluttered in, to flee, more frightened than before.

Against her lids the sun smouldered, throbbing redly through her head. The starling sent down a cacke of irritation from the eaves. She drew a deep breath slowly, drinking what little coolness was in the air; then she relaxed again, and let one hand rest limply on the grass, pretending that she did not have to think, that all that mattered was Harrison's new production which was shaping so very well.

The starling sniggered with a sharp tongue from the chimney-ledge, sarcastic and insincere.

Bishop found the third door along and knocked. It was ajar. Singing came from the other side, a cracked ditty cheerful and without tune. It grunted to words:

"Bowl in!"

Bishop bowled. The stout singer looked at him in the mirror above the long dressing-table.

"Hello. You looking for Balting?"

Bishop said, "Not particularly. Who's Balting?"

"The other denizen of this 'ere. Then you must be looking for me."

He went on washing his hands in the basin, his backside wobbling with effort. The plug chortled suddenly. As he swung round and whipped a filthy towel from a hook, Bishop offered his cigarette-case.

"Ah. Largesse! Insert here, please."

He thrust his face forward happily. Bishop lodged a cigarette between his lips and struck a match. The big hands busied themselves in the filthy towel, then it was slung to the dressing-table. The cigarette was jerked from its place with a quick hand; smoke was exhaled, luxuriously.

"First one this morning," he said. "Record? If you don't want to see Balting, you must want to see me. Or you've lost your bearings. If so I'll put you right."

He slid into a tweed jacket and smoothed his greying hair back in the mirror. Bishop lit his pipe at last and said: "I just wondered if Roy had turned up."

The big red hands stopped on their way across the greying hair; the bulbous blue eyes swivelled and fixed on the reflected face of Bishop.

"You a friend of his?"

"I wouldn't say that."

The man seemed to be waiting for a rider to that; but it was left floating in the air. He went easily to a shelf over the basin and got a small bottle down, and began rubbing the grease-paint off a collar with the spirit and a rag. The cigarette smouldered in his mouth as he talked.

"Roy," he said—and the cheerfulness had left his voice—"has hooked it. Didn't you know?"

Bishop moved carefully a tin of make-up cream and a tin clock from the end of the dressing-table, and perched one haunch there, looking down obliquely at the actor.

"Yes," he said. "I'm not sure, though, what sort of hook it was. I mean—did he have an accident somewhere?"

"It's all very odd, old boy. I'm Charles Molyneux, by the way, though I don't see how that helps."

"My name's Bishop." Then he remembered the most important thing that must be done when entering a dressing-room backstage. "I was out front a couple of nights ago. You made quite a memorable Mr. Hepple."

"Liked me? Oh good. Peach of a part, of course, can't go wrong." He shook the bottle again, blocking its neck with the rag. "No one knows about old Roy," he said, looking up with round eyes. "Saturday night two weeks ago he did two shows and seemed perfectly normal. Monday morning he didn't show up for rehearsals, and Monday night the A.S.M. had to go on. Case of thin air."

He swung his head as footsteps sounded down the passage, and called loudly, "Thomas!"

"Yep?" The footsteps slowed.

"Get my stuff?"

"Yep!"

"God bless you, my son!"

The footsteps went on, and a door opened somewhere at the end of the passage. Molyneux said, "Are you a kind of official?"

Bishop smiled gently. "No. I'm just interested in locating Roy, that's all."

He got a very straight look for a moment; then Molyneux went on with his cleaning, vigorously. "Oh. Well that's all I know about it, I'm afraid. Saturday night he was all right. Monday morning he was a gentle memory. The only thing was that his stuff was in quite a mess when I came in here just before rehearsals. I thought that queer."

"Stuff!"

A big hand gestured to the dressing-tables. "This stuff. I grant it's in quite a mess now, but you know what I mean. It had got knocked about, as though he'd dried on every line and come in here a paddy after the curtain. But that happens, sometimes. Last week I had 'flu and took six calls one night with a temperature of 102. When I left here, *my* stuff was in quite a mess, too. But Roy wasn't ill or anything. Strikes me as highly odd."

He held up the collar and observed it critically; the pungent tang of the spirit acidulated the air.

"Did Trafford have any worries?"

"Haven't we all? I don't think he'd do a thing like that, though."

"A thing like what?"

Molyneux looked up with a blank expression.

"Suicide. Isn't that what you meant?"

"No, but it's a thought."

The man grunted, rubbing the top of his

dressing-table with the spirity rag before he threw it away. "Does he owe you very much?" he asked casually.

"Not a cent. I just want to locate him. Thanks for what you've told me." He slid his haunch off its perch.

"It wasn't worth the cigarette—but thanks for that. Why don't you blow along and see Helen Ledine?"

"Might she know something?"

"More than I do, p'r'aps. Third door along and keep your trousers on, she's dynamite."

"Thanks."

"So-long. If you find Trafford, let me know. He owes *me* one and three."

Bishop went three doors along and knocked. A rich, feminine voice called:

"Male or female?"

In a deep bass Bishop said, "I vary."

"Oh. Two seconds."

He gazed at the oblong label on the door that said *Miss Helen Ledine—Miss Audrey Townend*. It was like a permanent introduction.

"All right!"

He went in. One of them was fifty and looked very arch although she was fully dressed. The other looked more dynamite and rather fetching in a risky wrap.

"Hello."

"Miss Ledine?"

"Even she."

The words came with a mechanical metallicness, as bright and as superficial as the nails she was crimsoning with Cutex.

The second half of the door-label smoked a cigarette, taking in the lean lines of the Savile Row ensemble and eyeing the contents with a smouldering, hooded gaze. Thirty years ago it might have worked.

Bishop said, "I've just been talking to Charles. He said I ought to come and see you."

"He'll get his ten per cent."

"About Trafford."

Posed in the long mirror, head lowered, one hand moving the brush, the other passive with the fingers spread, she was a study in concentration. Varnishing had to have that, or it was messy. But as he said Trafford's name she flicked a glance upwards and dropped it immediately, like a shutter. Yet the exposure had been long enough for her to take his expression. It was quite harmless.

"Roy Trafford?" she said slowly. The lights glared from above the mirror, tinting her auburn hair, highlighting her cheekbones, sheening across the satin of the blue wrap. One nyloned leg was crossed on the other, a sheer asset. "What about him?"

The voice had scarcely altered; apart from the camera-shutter glance she was unaffected; but her breathing had quickened.

"I wondered if you'd heard from him."

"When did you wonder? Between Charles' room and this one?"

"Yes. About seven and a half paces from his door, measuring from the handle."

"Bit elaborate. Would you have come to see me if Charles hadn't suggested it?"

"Eventually."

"When you'd dug my name up from somewhere else. Don't mind my accent, but a girl's got her reputation to think of. You see a lot of people think my relationship with Roy was solid. So when some-one asks about Roy they send him to me. Like Charles did with you."

"And was it solid?"

"Depends what you mean by solid."

"And what I mean by 'was.'"

Again she looked at him, a sudden flash of hazel and white. "He's missing, isn't he? To the tune of newsprint."

But Bishop was satisfied. It had caught her on the wrong foot. He needn't labour it. He said, "Can I smoke in here?"

"Does it go with Chanel? Because there's none around."

He lit the tobacco and dropped the match into the tin tray on the dressing-table. Miss Audrey Townend said, "You don't mind if I start making-up?"

"Shall I come back later?"

"Don't bother, it's just practice." She took off the jacket of her suit and slid a hanger into it. She then took off her blouse. Bishop thought somebody ought to tell her about the date. She'd forgotten her decades.

"Does Roy owe you enough to make you lose sleep?" Helen Ledine said easily. She screwed the top on the varnish-bottle and began waving her fingers slowly through the air, looking up at him with a straight stare.

"He doesn't owe me anything."

"You're just a friend of his."

"No. I'm trying to find him."

"Got your credentials?"

"Unofficially, that is."

She half-turned on the chair and leaned one elbow on the dressing-table, swinging the upper leg gently. Her throat had a white lustre and there was justification for good cleavage. Molyneux hadn't been fooling. She said in a low voice, "Why don't you ask Nicole where Roy is?"

He chose the last of the three alternatives that took a half-second to consider. Although Nicole had told him about Trafford, it would be an exception. She was a well-known producer's wife, and the West End had a healthy grapevine.

He said, "Nicole who?"

"Pedley. Roy's sleeping partner."

Miss Townend said shockedly, "Oh *dar*ling..." and went on giving her face a cream-base with mobile repercussion on the brassière.

Helen Ledine might not have realized the other woman was there at all. "If Nicole doesn't know where the boy is, who can? Not to speak too frankly."

She had lost, at last. There was an edge on her voice that shone, and every word honed it anew. Bishop fussed with his pipe, looking carefully at sea. "I don't think I ought to make this a general enquiry," he said. "I just came to see Charles, and as he suggested talking to you, and you were so close—well."

"Oh quite." They came out now in cut strips from her tongue. "Well, when you've seen Nicole and a few other people and come back full-circle, it'll be nice to have you drop in again."

He bowed slightly.

"Sorry to have bothered you."

"You didn't mean it."

He closed the door after him, shutting off the ice. When he got to the end of the passage he heard heel-clicks, loudening rapidly along the stone floor.

"It's not easy to talk sense with a third party doing a senile strip-tease," she said. Her voice was still edged, but deadly serious. "Meet you somewhere this evening?"

"Aren't you doing a show?"

"I mean afterwards. Preferably private—your place or mine?"

He said, "Make it mine. I'll pick you up here."

"Rather you didn't—what's your address?"

He told her and she just nodded and walked quickly back along the passage, leaving him with a hint of not-quite-subtle perfume and a feeling that by sheer chance he had saved himself much time. Helen Ledine was exactly the type of woman he had thought of since he had first seen Mrs. Pedley, and she fitted into the pattern that was forming already in his mind, like a plate in hypo.

To-night the image would sharpen, perhaps of a slayer's face.

5th

MOVE

AN EARL'S COURT DOUBLE-DECKER slid past the end of the lane and tipped out a pack of people, and, timing it just right, smothered them with diesel gas and rumbled off with a good belly-laugh. As they broke cohesion and drifted across the lane's end a taxi shuffled up and moaned with a bilious bulb. Some scuttled on, others hung back, the cab waited, the driver sat like a sack with a bland blank face saying, *make up your bloody minds will you* under his moustache; but there was no hurry. *What of this life if...* he stared at the girl with long blonde hair who loped across his radiator and reached the pavement with a long-thighed step.

The bus was out of sight, herded by others; the

cab went down the lane with a waxing clock and vanished into a mews. In the doorway of the jeweller's the man had not moved. Clouds were built in a brooding rampart against the late sun, and his face was shadowed. He watched the doorway opposite, twenty yards down the lane; but it was growing towards six o'clock and nobody wanted flowers or seeds as late as this: they were all off to see Jean Simmons and eat fish-and-chips, dine at the Dorchester and go on to the club.

The clouds were flung from Westminster to Hampstead, where the Heath sprawled like a great green rag among scattered bricks; and up the wide residential road the woman walked alone, walked easily and without hurrying. Then she came to the pillar-box and slid the letter in, and turned back, seeing for a moment the dull red painted cheeks of the ugly gnome, and the head that hung upside-down.

In Tallow Lane the man watched; in Hampstead the brief letter lay; the clouds ran down to the river and turned it grey. In a Chelsea window two eyes sat, burning as deep as sapphires, so luminously blue that the smoky fawn of the fur was a mere shadow with pointed ears. The cat stared at nothing in the dying of the day, and thought of little more, content simply to sit. Her name was the Princess Chu Yi-Hsin, but she did not know even that.

The man behind her was formulating a new contribution to the *Encyclopædia Britannica.* Last year he had dug from the earth in Peru a bone of curious shape, and had proved for a dozen learned men a theory they had held for decades. Others should know of this, and so he wrote his paragraph. The light of the desk-lamp glinted across his spectacles; their thick black sidepieces divided his head, separating the thin yellow hair and the doming brow from the tapering lines of the face.

The Siamese sat with the tranquillity that dwells in still water, soundless and immobile. The man wrote, building one accurate word upon another into an edifice that was dignified, informative and economical. In ten minutes he read the paragraph for the third time, and sat back, relaxing.

From the davenport below the Regency-stripe curtains that draped the adjacent wall, Miss Gorringe looked up.

"Explicit, Hugo?"

He nodded. "Yes. Shall we have a drink?"

She put down the doll she was making for the Children's Hospital and crossed to the cabinet. She asked:

"How deep?"

"Drownable-in."

She brought the glass and placed her own on the end of the desk, leaning back against the arm of a chair.

"Allah protect us," she said.

"Amen."

The Princess Chu Yi-Hsin stirred on the windowsill, and gazed round with slow eyes, delicate nostrils dilating to the scent of the sherry. Faintly through the windows there came a single hoot of a Thames tug.

Another ten minutes passed, for the wine was '34, a good year. When there was a thin brown lens of it left in the well of his glass, Bishop said:

"Your Highness."

The cat leapt, dropping to the desk with soft feet and a tail that flung out to aid balance and then curved round her haunches as she sat. He tipped the glass until the sherry welled to the rim; and she supped there with a small delicate tongue, afterwards gazing up into his face with the limpid sapphire eyes. He straightened the glass.

"Now scoot, you tipsy baggage, and don't let your father smell your breath."

The great eyes blinked drowsily over their Saturday-night delight; then she curled her fawn limbs in the middle of a chair and dismissed the company.

Bishop watched her for a moment, his eyes caressing the smoke-black ears, his mind relinquishing the sense of the paragraph he had just completed and circling selectively until it thought of the crimson nails, and the provocative wrap, and the voice that had become edged and taut.

"I've met a woman," he said, and lit his pipe.

Miss Gorringe looked at him. "Not that, not that," she murmured.

"By name—presumably professional—Helen Ledine."

"In Trafford's company?"

"That's right, at the Olympus. She's coming here tonight, after the curtain. Have you ever met her?"

"I've seen her on the stage."

"That's difficult. Quite a lot gets lost as it comes over the footlights. Let me sketch the lady for you. She is forty and looks thirty and is not so beautiful as rich in personality. A bit cheap, a bit drinky, a bit conscious that the fight's going to get tough from now on. She is also exceedingly interested in Trafford, to the extent—unless I'm wildly wrong—of either hate, love or both."

Miss Gorringe sounded pleased.

"She's the type we were looking for, isn't she?"

"Yes. I'm glad you said that. But the whole point is that Helen Ledine doesn't monopolise the pattern. She merely fits snugly into a vacant space. So we ought to view the whole thing, by the way of a sort of interim conference, before we try to see how important she might be."

"Shall I take notes?"

"Please. If only to keep you interested while I go into a very long monologue. Afterwards you can either file them or burn them, as you please."

She fetched her pad, choosing a straight-backed

chair that would keep her wits upright. Bishop hunched himself over the desk, letting the pipe hang down so that the smoke should climb from the bowl to his nostrils and there entrance him.

"Take four theories," he said. "One, that Trafford is alive; two, that he is missing by accident and not by design; three, that he has committed suicide; and four, that he has been murdered." His eyes narrowed, and focused on the chessboard. A pawn was about to block a rather cunning infiltration, and it distracted him slightly; he looked at Vera Gorringe instead.

"One: Trafford has deliberately bunked for reasons connected with money, Mrs. Pedley, or some unknown factor. What have we? In support—the letter that was sent to his lover from Tallow Lane: he is known to be broke, if not actually in debt: his dressing-table at the Olympus was left in a mess on Saturday night two weeks ago, according to the man who shared his dressing-room. Charles Molyneux."

Miss Gorringe looked up.

She said, "Why is that in support of theory number one?"

"Because it might have been following a violent scene with whoever was in the dressing-room late on Saturday night that he reached a decision to bunk—on the tide of a deep emotional upset. But of course the same factor might also support other theories."

She nodded, and added a few words to her pad. He said, "Theory number two, that he is missing by no choice of his own: I find that hard to credit. The only obvious answer to that one would be that someone is holding him against his will and calling the ransom blackmail. That's really a bit much to swallow, but we'll record it because one aspect might fit in with another theory. The third idea is suicide. Better, but still not good enough. He's an actor, therefore inclined to the emotionally dramatic—on the other hand sufficiently an egotist to want to go on living and not to be left behind while all his friends keep up the giddy whirl. However, suicide is a sort of delayed exhibitionism; they go out thinking of all the people who'll say well-I-never and I-should-have-understood-him-better and what-a-tragic-end-for-a-promising-genius—you know how these things go. That, I think, would fit his character rather well: but if he killed himself, who wrote the letter to Mrs. Pedley? Someone who knew of his death and is simply cashing-in on a charming afterthought? Improbable."

Miss Gorringe was not taking notes. She was selecting the salient points, and clearly didn't consider this one to be worth recording. Bishop noticed this. He said:

"The last of the main theories is that of murder."

He had said it slowly, because he was entering ground on which he felt more at home, less unsure.

Perhaps his tone had not changed, perhaps it had not been less loud; but Chu Yi-Hsing opened her eyes, and swung her head gently towards the desk and the man who sat there. He caught the movement, and returned the drowsy gaze.

"One note of Nellie Dean, you tippling hussy, and out you go." A shower of ash fell from his pipe, and he leaned back, pressing the tobacco down. "This has better possibilities. Did the outraged husband slay the infidel wife's lusty young lover? A little melodramatic, but not inconsiderable. However, I happen to know that Pedley was at home throughout that Sunday two weeks ago, and it seems unlikely that Trafford would have called there—he couldn't surely have wished to, particularly as Mrs. Pedley was away then. For which information, Gorry, much thanks. Where did you get it?"

"On a telephone," she said.

"All right, I don't want to know what my left hand's doing; it seldom does anything wrong. So much for the Pedley idea. What about the Other Woman? This might be more than a triangle. Mrs. Pedley is young and attractive and has a husband fifteen years her senior and physically unstartling—a triangle is therefore natural. But Roy Trafford is apparently good-looking to a degree, and to the kind of degree that magnetises the *mammalia*."

"Oh, come!" said Miss Gorringe, thinking she should.

"Use you own words but not block capitals. So that Trafford, being attractive, might have quite a retinue. Mrs. Pedley, for one. Helen Ledine for another. There could be more, but for the moment I'm interested in Helen. Still, we'll talk about her after she's been here to-night, when we shall know more."

"Do you want me here for an interview?"

"Rather not. Ledine is the type who lets her hair down more readily with an audience of one; and I want it right down."

"Very well, Hugo, about Mrs. Pedley—is she being absolutely straight with you?"

"No."

"Why not?"

"Because she's terrified of Pedley and desperately worried about Trafford. When a woman is both these things about anything she'll tell her closest confidante precisely what she thinks sounds plausible. Sometimes it happens to fit the truth. In this case I don't think she's done much serious lying, except about her last meeting with Trafford in the dressing-room at the Olympus."

"That's what made me wonder."

"I expected it would."

"What kind of a mess was the dressing-room in, did the Molyneux man say?"

"Make-up stuff, you know. Strewn about with lids off and things leaking—that's the impression I had from the little he told me. As though Trafford had been in a paddy, he said. With whom? Seemingly Mrs. Pedley. She gave me a full account of what was said and how they both reacted; but she might not have mentioned that he got a bit violently passionate and persuasive with her. She refused to telephone Pedley and stay the night in the West End with the boy-Casanova. She didn't say he was more than sulky about that. But it might account for the mess Molyneux found the place in."

"Why should she have it back from you?"

"Natural reticence."

"She tells you without much difficulty that she's being unfaithful to her husband and is being black-mailed by her missing lover—but she couldn't simply say to you something like, 'Oh, he got a bit angry and threw things about'?"

Bishop inclined his head sideways, raising his brows. "You may have something there—but women lie so quaintly and refuse to confess the oddest little things, out of sheer caprice. They're tricky critters."

Miss Gorringe smiled with studied affection.

"They are. This one is. She has you prejudiced after one talk. On her side."

"It's no good small-boying me. And I'm not saying she isn't holding things back and even trumping up some of the things she's told me; but I've a reason for thinking that she and Trafford did *not* have a shindy in the dressing-room. I think it might have been Ledine and Trafford."

"Ah." She said it with satisfaction. "The fourth corner of the quadrangle."

"Something like that, yes. Ledine might have gone back to the theatre. Mrs. Pedley's car was somewhere outside. Ledine might have noticed it, and—if she's as wild about Roy as I believe her to be—she might have got a fit of jealousy and gone back to lurk about until the Other Woman had left. Then to promote mayhem with her predatory male."

"Or she might have stayed in her own dressing-room until Mrs. Pedley had gone. Then ditto."

Her pencil was now moving all the time, and Bishop noticed that, too. "Even more likely. There's a further point here that we shouldn't miss—"

On the desk the telephone cut in. He picked it up. Miss Gorringe's pencil was poised. Chu Yi-Hsin lifted her head and yawned with closed eyes and a tensioned, curving tongue.

"Yes?"

"That you, Bishop?"

"Hello, Freddie. Still working?"

"I shall be working through to one o'clock."

"What about the Lord's Day Observance Society?"

Frisnay said something about the Lord's Day Observance Society and added:

"Look here, I've decided to let you know something that might be useful, in return for some of the ideas you gave me this morning."

"Good. Cast your bread, then."

"You can look at it like that, I suppose. Anyhow, it's this: Trafford got to his hotel—Sadler's in Arches Street—at about midnight on Saturday fourteenth. He wasn't alone. A porter heard an argument going on between about midnight and one o'clock; and about nine the next morning a woman slipped out of the hotel. He thinks she might have come from Trafford's room."

Bishop took a box of matches and gripped it between his knees and struck a match and lit his pipe and said:

"Well, well."

Miss Gorringe eyed him steadily.

"She was a brunette," Frisnay said. "That's all the man could say—except that in every other way she was 'medium' or 'average', which is what people tell you when they can't make up anything more sensational. But it's a lead." Frisnay allowed a lot of pause, and when it didn't bring anything he added: "Does all that interest you?"

"Excessively. I was thinking."

"Good. Incidentally, Bishop, just why d'you imagine Trafford is dead?"

Miss Gorringe saw him smile gently. His voice began purring like a Japanese diplomat's. "So..."

he said into the mouthpiece, "puzzled policeman, brooding in bewilderment upon startling statement made by astute friend earlier in the day, is forced at last to ring up and offer luscious tit-bit as cunning bait..."

"Oh, plurals," said Frisnay without heat. "I don't care what construction you put on it. Fact remains that it's perfectly true about the woman, and—"

"I know it is," honeyed Bishop gently, "in fact it's remarkable probable that this very medium-average brunette is taking liquor with me to-night, by appointment."

"The devil she is!"

"No, but quite a bitch, unless I'm wrong. However, I shall now fall into your wily trap and say simply that Trafford is very likely to be dead because he's blackmailing someone by letter."

There was another pause; then Frisnay grunted:

"But that's a paradox."

"Not at all. Trafford could blackmail this person just as easily *without* being missing. The fact that he begins the game almost immediately after fading out of everyone's ken suggests that someone is really doing it *for* him. Knowing damned well he can't do anything about it. Now all that, Frederick, is pure supposition. But if we don't eventually find that it's very close to the facts, I shall go and live in a cave with three purple parrots and a Tibetan mouse, gathering tubes of Spam from the woods for our food—"

"I don't know why I ever take any notice of you, Bishop."

"That has always puzzled me, too. It shows an intelligence beyond the capacity of an honest fellow."

"Will you let me know if you find anything out from your talk with the woman to-night?"

"I may. If it's nothing rude."

"Thanks," said Frisnay grudgingly.

"Think of it as simply nothing. Before you go back to torturing your office cat, tell me, have you got a man on the shop in Tallow Lane?"

"Yes."

"Any good?"

"Not so far."

"I'd keep him there, Freddie. I don't think he's wasting his time. 'Bye."

Frisnay grunted and hung up. Bishop said to Miss Gorringe, "Commence, please. Trafford believed to have taken woman to his hotel, midnight Saturday fourteenth. Porter heard argument in room between twelve and one. Woman seen leaving hotel about nine next morning, brunette, no description otherwise." When the pencil paused he added: "Our own note—may have been Helen Ledine or Mrs. Pedley, despite latter's denial of having stayed with Trafford that night."

"Useful," she said as she finished.

"Yes. The quaint thing about Freddie and me is

that he always thinks I'm helping him whereas the reverse is true. But don't tell him that, it'd spoil a beautiful friendship."

"Do you really think Mrs. Pedley stayed at the hotel, and didn't tell you?"

Bishop frowned at the scattering of ash on his desk.

"I don't know. But Helen Ledine will."

So quiet was the room that Hugo Bishop became aware of his own breathing, and the Princess Chu Yi-Hsin stared at him from the hearthrug with eyes so great and unblinking that there seemed almost a tangible conduit capable of carrying thought, even animal's to man. But the cat's gaze was not telepathic. She had turned her eyes to the only object in the room that ever moved, save when others were here.

Even Chu Yi-Hsin, knowing the man so well and knowing that he was not a noisy man, had perhaps wondered if he had fallen away with the rest of the vanishing world, so quiet was it here. Her blue eyes stared, and saw the man, and were satisfied.

Smoke climbed from the white pipe-bowl, a thin filigree vine that writhed and wavered upwards and upwards, fading before it could cling to whatever thing it sought in the fragile air. Bishop watched the pieces, his eyes as steady as the cat's.

The pieces were utterly still on the black and white squares; it seemed as though they would sit here until dusk settled, and cobwebs came; it seemed as though the white Rook would remain at his post, guarding the Queen and threatening the black Knight, for all time; it seemed as though the white King could now fall to sleep, or to death, no more fearful of the black Queen's threat, no more in dread of the black Bishop who was waiting five squares away, waiting with crabbed senile patience for the incisive diagonal thrust.

All these things, these fancies and these moods the silence gave to the room. Light was burning on, but time had stopped; time, and motion, and sound all ebbed away, leaving a final scene that would never change.

The small bright bell shattered the spell and flung its shrill clangour deep into the false dream of always-this.

Bishop's hand moved.

"Yes?"

"A Miss Ledine, sir."

"Send her up, please."

The telephone rattled back on to the sprung cradle and as though traffic had been released at the end of two minutes' silence a lorry rumbled through the street below and somewhere a car-horn voiced, echoed by bricks, and someone came singing a drunken song along the pavement of

King's Road. In the passage outside these rooms a lift-gate clattered open and within a moment clattered shut; the bell chimed its twin harmony as Bishop crossed the room. The head of the Siamese turned, watching his stride.

"Good evening," Bishop said. She came in quickly and the room became alive with her as her shadow fluttered along the wall from the wakened standard-lamp and her perfume bodied the air and her voice said:

"Hello. Did you expect me earlier?"

He looked at his watch.

"I'm afraid I haven't been watching the time."

"How nice not to have to."

He took her loose camel coat and as she slid out of it she half-turned her head and smiled up at him. Her eyes were large and very bright.

"How many calls?" he asked.

"Lots. I got quite giddy. Saturday-night crowd, of course." She moved slimly to the hearth-rug, looking down at Chu Yi-Hsin. "Other nights they start oozing in the middle of Act Three, can't say I ever blame them, it's more bloody than somewhat. Magnificent cat."

"She never gets up for anyone, sorry." He opened the flap and the concealed lamps glimmered on, flowing against the mirrors. "What would you like to start with?"

"Is it going to be an orgy?"

"If you feel like one."

"Then I'll break down the polish with pink gin."

"Cigarettes behind you."

"Thanks."

The Siamese got up and stretched, tensioning the length of her fawn limbs in a vibrant curve with claws hooking into the pile; then she sat, relaxing, nostrils slightly curious about the strange perfume.

Bishop gave the woman her grin and raised his Martini.

"Lady Diana," he said. It was her part in the play.

"Thank you."

He bent down and lit the gas-poker beneath the coal and log in the hearth. "Sorry, I should have done this earlier. I've been dreaming."

"Hashish?"

"No, just thinking soberly upon matters. Is that gin all right?"

"Heavenly." She held the cigarette aside so that the smoke should clear them; it was as though she were making an appealing gesture with one hand, for she was also watching his face, slightly amused, slightly curious. He thought, too, slightly nervous. She was waiting for him to begin; and he was not going to do that. She said, "It's lovely weather we're having, for this time of year."

"Isn't it?"

"So—so seasonable." She found the right expression with perfect pretence, and finished with a nervous little giggle.

"After such a winter, too," he murmured, sipping his drink. She drew a deeper breath, and her hazel eyes narrowed a fraction.

"Very well. Can I know why you're so interested in Trafford?"

He raised an eyebrow. She had switched too suddenly from the tentative to the direct. It was meant to be amusingly frank. He found it frankly amusing.

"Yes. Because he's missing."

The gas-poker flared, sending up blue banners between the idle logs; its breath gasped in the quiet room.

"You're interested in that?"

"Of course. West End actor mysteriously disappears."

"People do that every day. D'you get interested in all of them?"

"No." The monosyllable dropped like a flat doughnut; and her eyes fired despite her poise.

"D'you get a sore throat, chattering away like that?"

"My dear woman, you asked me to meet you tonight, and with not the slightest prompting on my part. And here we are. If your idea was to spend half an hour over cocktails, then I couldn't be happier. You'll find that as a host I'm a bit vague but honest in my intention to make the whole thing go with a gay old swing. But if you had any more serious reason for meeting me, I can't be expected to pump you for it. Why should I?"

She said, "That was quite a load off you mind."

"It didn't weigh very heavily."

She was growing angry, faster than she wanted to; and he was pleased. Anger was a stimulant; and people in their emotional cups spoke so much more freely, and spoke more truth.

"Are you some sort of private eye?"

"Would you translate?"

"American. It means private investigator, detective, enquiry agent, snooper, keyhole-tout, a rat that gets paid for raking up dirt with his nose. Am I explicit?"

"Perfectly. More so in English than in American."

"You've no idea what fun it means to be bilingual. But don't let me lead you from the point. Are you?"

"A private eye? No. Private, yes, and in my fonder moments a visionary, but never quite both."

He added, "Excuse me," and turned off the gas-poker. A few flames had been born among the coal and the peeling bark of the logs. The hissing stopped. "We don't want to be too warm, do we?" he said, straightening up. She stood quite still, tilting her gin. She was already warmer than she had intended to become, and that increased her anger.

The man had a nerve, strolling into her dressing-room and asking her about Roy. Asking Charles Molyneux, too. Who was he, this damned abusive Pimpernel?

"I admit this is my party, even though we haven't been decently introduced." She had pared the edge off her voice, but it was left slightly raw.

"Does that matter?"

"Oh, yes. For one thing I had to give the porter below your flat number. He looked at me with cork-screw eyes. For another thing you might be my laundry man's girl-friend's pawnbroker. That'd be embarrassing."

She moved casually round the room, looking up at the Manet and holding her hands behind her, the cigarette between two fingers.

"My name is Bishop, and I do not pawnbroke."

"You're too sensitive, it's quite fun." She reached the small triangular table near the desk, and stooped with her back to him, turning the pages of the directory that was there. Her back looked slinky in the peach linen suit. He drained his Martini and said:

"You'll find it under the B's."

"You don't mind?"

"Why should I?"

"Some people don't like the visitors looking at their books."

"It isn't mine, it's the G.P.O.'s. To save your diligent investigation. I could show you my driving-licence."

"It's all right, I've found it. So your name is really Bishop. What's F.A.S.?"

"Fellow of the Archæological Society. Old bone-digger-uppers, you know."

"A grave undertaking." She turned, and browsed over the chessboard on the great limed-oak desk.

He said, "Tell me if you will, what did you *think* my name might be, before you asked?"

She looked up, over her shoulder, smiling

"I hadn't a clue. But I didn't think you were one of the people interested in Roy Trafford. I imagined I knew all their names. You're a new one. You say you're not a detective and perhaps I believe you. Are you anything to do with the police?"

"Only when I race the lights."

"So you ride a bicycle, too. As well as play chess." She came down the length of the room, walking beautifully. She walked as a cat might, stalking. "You're playing chess with me, aren't you? Well I've made my gambit and it's Bishop's move. Why don't you?"

"It's a curious gambit. It has me puzzled."

"It's simpler than you think. I asked you if we could meet to-night because Roy was a great friend of mine. He was also my lover." Her voice had become, suddenly, a low monotone; and for the first time he thought she was speaking without guile. "So when a strange man drifts into my dressing-room and asks about him, I'm interested in who he is, and what he wants, and what *he* knows about Roy."

She stopped walking, and stood within a pace of him, her head tilted upwards to let her eyes meet his. "That's natural," she said, "you must admit. So I came here to ask you: what *do* you know about Roy?"

Bishop met her eyes. As he began talking he entered ground that would support him only if he trod with supreme caution. But the advantage was with him. Ledine did not know him or his name, so far as any link with Trafford was concerned. She had no clue to his interest in the affair. She was, even at this moment, talking in the dark to a stranger. This allowed him to probe her mind more deeply than if she knew where the scalpel was going; but if he touched a naked nerve...

"I can't answer that without involving you," he said softly, "so perhaps I ought not to try—"

"Don't worry about me. I'd like to know."

"Very well. Stop me if I become impudent. The chief thing that interests me about Roy is the subject—you understand I must speak carefully—the subject of the quarrel you had with him on Saturday night."

He pulled out his tobacco-pouch, which he knew to be empty, and peered into it, frowning. Her tone was as quiet as a taut steel wire.

"Saturday night?"

He nodded, crossing to the desk and filling his pipe from the tobacco-jar. He preferred not to face her so intimately when he was striving to break down the tissue.

"That's right," he murmured. "Two weeks ago. At Sadler's." The little scalpel stopped. There must be reaction before probing on. It came.

"When did he tell you about that?" She was quietly furious; not, he sensed, with him so much as with Trafford.

"Well," he said, breaking the tobacco-strands and putting the lid on the jar, "he didn't have much time to tell me *after* Sunday morning. Did he?"

As he came slowly back to the hearth he saw her silhouetted against the flushing logs. Her hands were in front of her now, and the cigarette was restive in her fingers; it had lost its roundness; ash had fallen, and she had not noticed. On a chair near by, the cat was curled, eyes wide open as she was aware of the quietness that had come back to the room; but now there was an undercurrent of tension that was tangible to the three of them, mostly acutely, perhaps, to the animal.

"Why in hell," the woman breathed, "should he have told you about it? Is it your business?"

"It is not."

"Then why should he tell you?"

"I can't imagine."

"It's utterly personal."

"I agree. If you remember, I said a moment ago that I couldn't tell what I know about Trafford without involving you. But you said I wasn't to worry. Now that you see what I meant, I'll stop."

With a desperate stillness she said:

"I think you've gone a little far to stop there. Do go on, I'm so intrigued."

"All right, since you ask." He turned away. "Shall we begin round two with the same again?"

Her voice followed him softly to the cabinet.

"Thanks, but I want to stay sober."

He poured himself another cocktail with a polite shrug, turning back with the glass in his hand.

"You make it sound so serious," he murmured.

"And isn't it?"

"Very." And he realized with a feeling of slow satisfaction that by "it" she meant something that she was now sure he knew about. It might be only another step to make that false impression a fact. "Very serious indeed," he said, his scalpel moving tenderly. "So perhaps you see now that this thing is bound to intrigue me, as well as you. It has so many—implications, hasn't it?"

Her face was not still; her eyes reacted to every word as though they were reading them on a screen; and her patience broke, as he had hoped it would, before he had finished, before he had to think of other vague phrases that gave nothing away.

"How much in love with Nicole are you?" she said, and her voice revealed how intuitive she thought she was.

His mind circled, selected the link, secured it, and used its strength immediately.

"Perhaps not at all. You mentioned her name to me—"

"Yes, in the dressing-room. But then we weren't alone. I couldn't talk properly, nor could you. Now you can admit you know which Nicole I mean." She was on the tide of a new certainty; that she had found out who he was, at last. Not a stranger in the darkness but another young man in love with the Pedley woman. "Was it a shock to you, Mr. Bishop, when I referred to her as Roy's sleeping partner?"

"Not entirely."

"I'm glad. I hate to see men hurt; they can't take it, as we can." She talked now with less nervousness, more intimately now that she knew who he was. There was also a note of slight triumph in her voice. "Mr. Bishop, you're really not in the least complicated after all."

"Good. I'd much rather be like an open book."

"Oh, you're all of that. A French novel, teeming on every page with unbridled emotions, ill-considered actions—stop me if I read too loudly."

"Please go on, you're quite amazingly psychic—"

"No, not exactly that, but a woman, with a brain. That's a formidable combination. The funny thing about this little affair is that you and I are in roughly the same boat—or were, until you killed Trafford."

She waited, her eyes faintly amused, watching

him sideways through the smoke of her cigarette. Bishop's face was blank; he didn't say anything. She said: "Don't you want to deny that?"

"Why should I"?

She shrugged. "I'm glad you don't." Slowly the amusement was leaving her eyes; her head was turning, and when she spoke again her voice was shorn of any expression but a strange, half-fearful admiration. "Mr. Bishop, I've never met anyone quite so magnificently callous. It's the conception of a very subtle mind, and perhaps only a woman with a murdered lover could see the truth of things."

From the chair, the Princess Chu Yi-Hsin watched the quiet-voiced woman. From the wide stone hearth, flames writhed and flew to the chimney's throat and sap sang in the logs' cracks. Helen Ledine watched the man, and in her face was fascination.

"But what about your boss, Mr. Bishop? Won't you have to kill him, too, before you're through? First the lover, then the husband—and the woman's yours." The words ebbed to a whisper, and the hazel eyes narrowed, and her breathing quickened. "You'll never tell me, but it's fun to ask ... just how long has Pedley got to live?"

6th
MOVE

 THE CAT STARED.

Each wide eye was great and deep with blue, an intense blue that came from nowhere, because the globe was transparent as a gipsy's crystal. In the round blue globe the figures moved, the man's and the woman's, their reflected images like actors on a screen. They were facing, and between them they held a bright black ball. That was the pupil of the cat's eye. They did not know they held it between them.

The woman was in pink, a peachy pink that toned most beautifully with the blue limpidity of the cat's eye iris. Her hair was dark brown, curtaining her profile. Her arms were bare from the wrist to the elbow; the skin was clear, the line slim.

The man was much taller than she, and the straw-fairness of his hair lightened the blue of the prism that contained him, embraced him intimately with the woman. It was the man who was speaking now.

The cat stared. The words reached the soft black ears, but not intelligibly, for she was only a cat. So that as the two figures stood facing in the mirror of each blue eye, and spoke, it was as if the sound-track of the film ran backwards in a stream of gibberish.

"Is all that in American again?"

"But no. Simple English, this time."

"That's odd. I don't understand a word."

"No?"

"Should I?"

"Of course. You, more than anyone."

"Oh. I must say you expect rather a lot."

"But I said so little."

"I agree, but a little gibberish goes a long way. D'you think we could take it bit by bit? It sounds very interesting, phonetically."

"You're wasted, off the stage, Mr. Bishop."

"First name's Hugo. Less frigidly formal than the other—considering you've been informal enough to accuse me of murder."

"Hugo, then. I like it. Slightly pompous, but unusual."

"Good. Now I'd rather like to know something.

You said what about my boss. His name?"

"Harrison Pedley."

"And the nature of my work for him?"

"The removal-business. Hotel-to-mortuary service. Charges for unwanted actors a little higher, owing to the risk involved."

"Yes, of course. But why should I remove Trafford for Pedley's sake?"

"Perhaps you volunteered. For a fee."

"Because I'm desperate for money?"

"No, judging by this exquisitely furnished room; but the wealthiest men are known to surprise their friends by appearing in the bankruptcy court one fine morning. Perhaps you suggested that to Pedley."

"But why, if it were only a suggestion? I assure you it wouldn't be true."

"I don't believe for a moment it would. But you could still make Pedley believe it."

"My reason?"

"Your infatuation for Mrs. Pedley."

"Sorry, but even if that existed I don't understand why I should kill her lover and ask her husband for the fee."

"It isn't very complicated. The fee is—due to your requesting it for allegedly mercenary reasons—promised. The work is executed, in a way certain to implicate Pedley, though you didn't make that clear to him. After the execution you refused the fee."

"How generous of me."

"On the contrary. You took care to see that, in the event of discovery, Pedley would be the scapegoat, leaving you in the clear."

"That must have been very clever of me."

"You are a clever man."

"Almost superhuman."

"No, just inhuman. A moment ago I said that I'd never met anyone so magnificently callous, that Roy's death was the conception of a subtle mind. This is why I said that. After Roy was dead and the fee refused, you were in a unique position. Nicole's lover was out of the way. Her husband—carefully framed for what he agreed you should do for him— was in your hands. Now you could draw the fee that you'd had in mind from the beginning. Pedley's divorce."

Bishop realised suddenly that he had quite forgotten something. The Martini in his hand. So he drained it, and moved to the cocktail cabinet, setting the glass down. It made no sound, because there was a slight film of spilled liquor on the mirror-base, and a suction cushion was formed beneath the concave bottom of the glass.

When he turned, Helen Ledine was taking another cigarette from the box. He fished for his matches but she said, "It's all right," and pressed her lighter. On the low padded chair the cat had gone to sleep. The blue eyes had closed and the magic figures had left their screens; the sound-track was running-on, but did not reach the depths of the feline dream.

As Bishop came back to Ledine, he walked very slowly, and his hands hung at his sides. His eyes were fixed on hers with a strange intensity.

"My dear Helen," he said softly, "if what you say is true, my position seems to be in jeopardy." He stopped, almost touching her, and looked down with his head slightly sideways, his eyes narrowing. "Doesn't it?"

Her head lifted; she didn't look away; but the cigarette began writhing whitely between her fingers and the lamplight flared across the crimson nails.

"You needn't worry about me," she said. "I've kept greater secrets than that."

His tone was silken. His stare widened, and, almost imperceptibly his shoulders were beginning to move, to lift, as his arms flexed and the hands opened, finger by finger. For a moment she was not aware of this; then her gaze was broken and she looked down and saw the hands, looked up with eyes suddenly wide, and saw his expression.

"But can I rely on that, my dear?" he murmured gently.

"Of course." She said it with a tight throat and an urgency that squeezed past her control. "Of course you can rely on it. I shan't say a word—why should I?"

His hands were still moving, so slowly that they were like an automaton's overcoming inertia with a sluggish strength. Again the hazel eyes flashed down, flashed up, and they were afraid. The hands lifted, with the fingers spread: she had looked down at them, away from his face, and now she looked up at it, away from these hands.

"Bishop—Hugo—please don't be absurd, I—shall forget everything as soon as I leave this—"

"Yes..." The answer was over-sibilant. "I think it would be better that you should, Helen. Forget everything, and be silent, always..."

As she stepped backwards her heel caught the edge of the rug and she pulled up with a jerk from her throat. Her eyes were luminous and could no longer look away from the expression in his face. A queer half-smile lay along his mouth and his stare was bright, and fixed, and somehow fascinated.

"Hugo!" Her voice pitched and broke, a strident reed that was snapped in the bitter wind. Blood had fled her face and in her hand the cigarette had bent, so that a few amber strands showed up through the riven paper. "Hugo—I'll do anything you ask!"

His hands dropped and the strange light left his eyes and he turned away, taking his pipe from the shelf and prodding the ash down. His voice was perfectly level.

"Good. Then get yourself a new cigarette, you

need it. Sorry I put the wind up you, but it was necessary." He lit his tobacco and flicked the dead match into the hearth. "This time I prescribe a brandy and ginger-ale."

The glasses clinked in the cabinet; he selected their drinks and looked at her over his shoulder. "Like a cheese-straw, Helen?"

She was statuesque on the rug's white pile; the colour was back to her face.

"Damn—your—*eyes*," she said in her throat.

He turned his head, shrugging, taking up the two glasses. "Oh. Must say I've never had my cheese-straws turned down quite so emphatically."

Her colour was back and her eyes were no longer wide and afraid, but under the peach linen the out-line of her breasts lifted and fell, and the breathing was tremulous. She had thrown the broken ciga-rette into the logs. When he offered her the brandy and ginger-ale he thought for an instant that she would dash it from his hand; but he was wrong. She took it, eyeing him fixedly.

"Thanks. To the finest ham-actor off the stage."

He smiled pleasantly.

"Thank you. To the supporting role."

The hazel eyes flared but she said nothing. Of this he was glad. She had been persuaded to say a little too much, and now she would speak only when she had selected and groomed a few exact phrases. That gave him a moment in which to think.

Her accusation had been childish. He could have broken down the fabric of the theory time and again, as she had woven it aloud. But the theory and the charge were not worthless. During her wild and melodramatic challenge, Helen had revealed a knowledge of facts and of people that Bishop wanted for himself. He had simply to shift the gravel diligently to come upon the infrequent but precious nugget.

He sipped his cocktail, gazing at the flames. She said to him:

"Was that for fun?"

His head turned.

"Was what?"

"Your act. Student of Karloff?"

"No. But you said I was a murderer. I didn't know whether you really believed it, or if you were cooking it all up for some reason. I had to find out, so I just played it your way; and you were afraid. You really believed you were alone in this room with a murderer. I'm sorry I frightened you. Please forgive me."

His voice was very quiet and sincere. His long grey eyes held no amusement. For a moment he was like a rather charming small boy who was confessing to a broken window.

She looked down, suddenly, at her brandy, and when she had lowered it again she said ruefully, "My God, you're like a bloody chameleon."

"Mean I'm stuck at red?"

Her smile was reluctant, but it came.

"No. I mean you're like that emotionally. You scare the skin off my spine and the next minute you're asking to be forgiven, in the sort of way that's not easy to refuse. Damn you Hugo, I still don't know who you are or what you are, even though you've thrown me bodily round the room and stood me up again with a brandy in my hand."

He shrugged.

"Sorry that's how it felt. I mean no 'arm, lady."

She gave him a slow glance and drew a breath deeply.

"You're utterly infuriating. I ought to hate your guts."

He began walking up and down, because the fire was warm and he wanted to think, and the habit was peripatetic.

"Helen," he said evenly, "ninety per cent of the sum total of ineffable poppycock and balderdash you've just fabricated is of course as true as a schoolboy's excuse. Even taking into consideration that you've probably been born, weaned and nurtured in the theatre, your picture of me as a double-dyed super-Bluebeard is wildly theatrical if not downright funny. But the ten per cent shows more intelligence."

"Don't mince your words for my sake, darling."

"I won't. This ten per cent concerns Nicole Pedley, and my alleged infatuation with her."

His shadow flickered across the wall, a lean ballet-figure that danced attendance on its live original. From the chair the Princess Chu Yi-Hsin watched his moving, her smoky head turning lazily.

"That theory," he said, "is quite reasonable. I've lumbered into this little affair, unnamed and unannounced. Nicole appears to be the only cause." He waved his pipe, sketching a pennant of grey-blue smoke across the lamplit air. "Well, I'm neither denying nor admitting anything. Think what you like about that."

He stopped, looking down for a moment at the pieces on the chessboard, his back was turned to Helen.

"Thanks," her voice floated up the room.

He swung round. "You're welcome. But the point's this: why did you drag murder into it?" He was walking back now, slowly towards her with a wrinkled brow.

"Because I think Roy is dead."

"Yes?"

"Don't you?"

"Perhaps."

She moved her slim shoulders an inch. "Then we seem to agree on something, for all my sad lack of intelligence."

"Put your claws in, Helen, they spoil the ensemble."

"I might need them again, any minute. You're a fraction unpredictable."

"Supposing Trafford is dead—don't you feel . . . a bit upset?"

"Very."

"But scarcely prostrated."

"C'est la vie."

"But you're not the philosophical type."

"I practise as best I can."

"Can I say personal things again?"

"After what's gone before, I think you could say almost anything and leave me unscathed."

"Very well—you're not terribly upset about the idea of his being dead because you were going to lose him in any case. Kindly mark with a tick or cross as applicable."

"I like your nerve, but it works. Yes. I was going to lose him anyway. So?"

"In fact it isn't a bad answer to the whole thing, is it? You've offered me a reason for my having killed the boy. I can give you a reason less elaborate, a reason for your doing precisely the same thing. On that night when you had a row with him in his dressing-room and another in the hotel, you were watching him make the final break. Soon he would go to Nicole, for good. But—presuming he became missing due to death—after that Sunday, neither of you could have him. It was stalemate; and that was better than defeat."

Her poise had returned. It had been shattered by fear of him, by his own deliberate trick; it had swung from fear to relief, from relief to a reluctant admission of his charm; now it had steadied and was stabilised.

"You think I killed Roy, rather than let Nicole have him?"

"No. I think you may have; and, if you did, I think that was your motive."

"Trifle French."

"France hasn't the monopoly of the *crime passionel*. The idea just began there, and it's an idea acceptable to anyone in the world, given the right temperament, the right passion, the courage and the opportunity."

"Mind if I quote you?"

"If it's selective."

"Very. Well, I'm neither denying nor admitting anything. You can think what you like about that."

"Word-perfect."

"It's my job."

She put her empty glass on to the shelf over the hearth; her brown hair swung a little as she turned back, throwing her cigarette away. She spoke softly. "That, I should imagine, brings us to the end of Act Three. Do we have the pleasure of a curtain-speech?"

"Of course. Thank you so very much for coming along. I hope you have enjoyed the evening."

She moved from the hearth-rug, towards him.

"And will come again?"

With her hands clasped naïvely behind her she looked up at him, head tilted, hazel eyes slow-lidded, perfume provocative.

"And will come again," he nodded gently.

She waited, with perfect timing, until she knew that he was not going to accept the invitation of her lifted face, and left herself with a second to withdraw. A moment longer, and a rebuff would have become tacit.

"Thank you," she said. When he opened the door for her she half-turned and smiled sweetly. "When you see Nicole, say how sorry I was not to give her my lover. But give her at least my love. Good night Hugo."

Her perfume was still in the room, when he turned the switch of the standard-lamp and murmured a word to the Siamese. Her perfume was still in the lift, when he closed the gates and pressed the contact for ground-floor. Her perfume was not in the open street, but he went on to the pavement and, for an instant, paused.

A Bentley slid along the kerb and turned left at the lights ahead. A double-decker bus passed across his vision, blotting out four shops at a time, and then three, and then one, until it was like a small red box in the street's distance.

Past Paultons Square a woman was walking, towards Church Street. She was not hurrying. Her camel coat swung as she went beneath the lamps.

He struck a match, and lit his *meerschaum*, and begun to make his way along the still-warm pavement, past the shrubs to Paultons Square. The tobacco-smoke skirled behind him, faint, and blue, and as frail as a drifting web along the warm night air.

7th

MOVE

OPERATION METROPOLIS: ZERO HOUR.
In London the garrison woke to sunshine. As they brought milk in and broke their shoe-laces, the invasion began, a movement that gathered its momentum from far away, from the outermost fringe of a gigantic circle.

They came with watches synchronised, and joined at the prearranged centres of rendezvous, phalanx upon phalanx of massed battalions that stormed the transports in Purley and points south, Ponders End and points north, Dartford and points east; and a few detachments hurried in from the west; the weakest flank.

The main spearheads attacked Victoria, London Bridge, Waterloo and Charing Cross, but there was no opposition save for the bottlenecks at the barriers. Once through, many of the forces broke free from the main contingents and paraded in single-file by the tobacconists' counters, awaiting their ration of nicotine, for this was vital to such an army. Later, the second most vital sinew for their strength would be drawn at each group-garrison: tannin, taken diluted and at approximately 85 degree Centigrade.

They had rested, the day before. Some were not changed; they had lain in a deck-chair on a lawn, had washed the Austin, had gone to church. Others—the minority—had changed without yet knowing it; they had hastened to Brighton and had allowed the young man a greater privilege than they had intended, they had gone too fast in the country lane and only the urgency of this morning's invasion had got them from bed with light abrasions, they had visited Aunt Margaret and found her unwell even considering her great age and problematical form of will. Others—the smallest group of all—had changed and were aware of it; they realised that yesterday's show-down with the wife had been more terrible than any before and boded a final breach, they realised that what Jones had told them between the fourth tee and the sixth green could only mean that the firm was down to the gunwales and there'd be a sacking due, they realised that Mary's morning upsets must now mean what they had hoped for at last: and Monday was a miracle.

So that there was nothing stereotyped about these million units of the invasion, except their massed onslaught. They were still individuals, and their problems were peculiar to each. By nine-thirty the attack was over. Positions had been gained on schedule. The tumult was not dispersed, but concentrated in a hundred thousand offices and buildings.

London steadied, sated with reinforcements. Time came in which to think coherently. Phone-calls had gone out on Saturday; this morning their effect was seen. Letters had been posted on Saturday; this morning they were received.

They were not all concerned with business. One letter, that had lain among others in a Hampstead box, was now franked and less pristine. It had gone from box to sack to van to counter to van to sack ... and had slipped through the small oblong mouth of a door in Tallow Lane.

It lay now, with three others, across the corner of a seed-box. It was addressed to R. B. Trafford Esq. During the day, the little courteous man put it into a slightly larger envelope, and, before evening, posted it. The name of the addressee was of course different.

———

On the morning of Tuesday, everything began again, like a vast joke the exact point of which had been lost. London woke with bloodless arteries and vacant cells; but by nine-thirty the streets were jammed, the buildings bloated anew. And the letter that had gone from Hampstead to South Kensington was now in the West End.

The larger envelope was slit open with a paper-knife; the blade slashed again, and the letter was taken out. It was not a long one. It said

> Roy,
> I *must* see you.
> N.

For some minutes the man sat thinking. There was no direct sunlight in the room, but radiance flowed through the windows from the buildings across the street; his eyes were bright with this warm, diffused light as he sat in the chair and thought. And when he had finished, he slipped a sheet of notepaper into the typewriter, and replied to the letter. The message was as brief, but she would understand.

The man was a little annoyed with her. There had been no cheque, either with her own signature or that of Harrison Pedley's. But he was fair enough to blame himself partly for this. He should have asked less than two hundred pounds in the first instance, and more than fifty pounds in the second. He was not used to this sort of thing. One must obey certain natural laws, certain demands of simple psychology. First, fifty; then perhaps seventy-five; then a hundred, and so on. It was much more reasonable. The screw must turn slowly, not come down with a sudden twist and then release.

He tucked his letter into a plain white envelope that bore Nicole Pedley's typed name and address, and put it into his pocket-book. Before this evening he would post it in South Kensington, so that the post-mark would be right.

The letter would make her very happy, for a while. For a few hours she would know relief from wretchedness. He had allowed her that, in the few words of his reply. He was a most saintly man who left the sunless room, and went down the flight of stairs, humming a tune.

On the morning of Wednesday, the gigantic joke was played again, but nobody laughed. They had no time; they jumped on just as the guard blew the whistle; they squeezed on when the conductor said *one more*; they were stacked, packed, guarded and conducted to their single destination—the sprawling ramparts of granite built on gold and black with smoke, the inland resort that never had to advertise: London-on-Thames.

A million letters had been shuffled through the night by men with nothing up their sleeves; a thousand had been scattered throughout Hampstead's morning roads; and among the half-dozen on the breakfast-table, Mrs. Pedley found the one that she could not open now.

When Harrison lifted his coffee-cup she slipped the letter aside and out of sight. The others lay on the lace between the toast-rack and the flower-bowl; and the small fingers moved in a moment, opening them. The early sunshine gleamed across the *Dark Fire* of her nail-colour. The paper ripped.

It didn't matter. Why open them? They wouldn't mean a thing. Beside the other one they were like whining little circulars among an invitation to a Royal Ball. Whatever they said, she wouldn't care. The other was there.

Pedley looked up from his own pile. It was larger, but of little more interest.

"Lots of fun, Nicole?"

"M'm?"

"Gay invitations to the rightest parties?"

"Oh. Not quite. You remember Susan?"

"The girl with plaits?"

"She had then. Now she wants me to open her new salon for her in a fortnight's time. Bond Street and giddily *à la*."

"Salon for what?"

"Oh, beauty things."

"Good. Most appropriate choice. Except that your presence there will disprove the very thing she's trying to sell people."

She smiled, forcing herself.

"Darling, I could cry when you pay me compliments. They're so terribly involved—but very sweet. Have you got lots of fun in yours?"

"Some. That young man Gilison's agreed to come up from Stratford without a rest."

"I should say he has! Chance of a lifetime for him."

"I know, but he's had a gruelling season."

"He hasn't started yet—what are you giving him?"

"*Autumn Gold.*"

"Is Tony doing that for you?"

"I think we shall do it jointly, but I've left the casting to him—with a few suggestions. I had a bright idea on Saturday, and he phoned me last night, agreeing."

"He's a nice little man. What did he agree to?"

"Helen Ledine. I told you she came to me for some work on Saturday—"

"But didn't you say you had nothing for her?"

His smile was slightly mischievous as he saw her expression. It was of unpleasant surprise, and for the first time she was really taking notice of what they were saying; for this moment the South Kensington postmark was forgotten.

"Dear, sweet, Nicole, you must learn to like my leading-ladies—some of them may be bitchy but they all work like Amazons."

He stirred his coffee, leaving a faint smile of amusement on his plump bland face.

"You—you mean she has the lead in *Autumn Gold*?"

"I told her I'd nothing for her, but at lunch I had the idea, and telephoned her, telling her to see Tony."

For a moment she said nothing; then shrugged.

"I can't say I'd have expected him to agree to that, my dear. Still, you're the king."

"Tony is no fawning sycophant, no sly-tongued sophister." He was utterly at ease and quoting light-heartedly. "What exactly is it that raises my lady's pretty hackles when Helen's name—?"

"Oh nothing," she said too quickly, too loudly. "Just an absurd intuitive dislike—temperamental maladjustment or whatever other label suits the case."

"Darling, you have just become guilty of one of the most atrocious puns ever to be cast across the breakfast-table. Any more of that sort of thing, and—"

"'Pologise—I apologise. Unintentional." She closed her eyes for a moment, smoothing the lids with cool fingers. It was too much. Trivial word-play could be amusing with Harrison and a few friends. Among company he developed form, expanded, was a brilliant wit. But within an hour of getting out of bed it was not the same. She sat as a target for his wit—and his wit was poor first thing in the morning. A sort of habit.

"Headache?" he asked gently.

She had been getting headaches, for the past fortnight. It was just the hot weather. It was an apt excuse.

"No, dear. The sunlight's a bit dazzling. Eyes aren't awake yet." They opened, and she smiled. "Harrison, you must find me an insufferable bore at breakfast-time. I'm so sorry!"

"But, my dear!" He got up and came round the table slowly, admiring the picture she made against the carved chair-back, the dark oak panelling behind it that sharpened the line of her shoulders, her lifted face, her hair. "Of all things," he murmured quietly, "never a bore. A beauty, perhaps, a delight, a study in repose by Crisseau—"

"You're too sweet to me," she said quickly, raising her hand. He mustn't go on. She was a bitch, a whore, an ingrate; she sat here to receive gracious compliments from a tender man, sat here with her lover's letter out of sight.

He took her hand, and kissed it. She had offered it, hoping he would. Otherwise he would have gently kissed her cheek, or brow; and his lips were fleshy and overfull, his skin was pale and scraped by the recent razor, his neck formed a white roll over the edge of his collar. Loving what was so gentle in the man, so tender and affectionate, so husbandlike, she would have seen only the white skin and the bulging neck. Admiring sincerely and intensely the poetry and art that formed this man, she would have felt only the fleshy pressure of the lips, the heat of the blood that had no warmth for her.

He held the cool hand, caressing it, while she sat unmoving and unmoved, filled only with a hideous wonderment that he was so close to her and knew nothing of her pity, revulsion, impatience to be free from him so that she could shred the envelope and tug out the letter and read...and read...It would scarcely matter what the words said; he might ask for money, or for help; he might—if miracles were—say that she could see him, as she had asked. But it wouldn't matter. The letter would be from Roy; it would be a thread, however fragile.

Harrison Pedley straightened up, for a moment stroked her hair, and went back to finish his coffee. As he pressed a cigarette into his ebony holder she said:

"Will you want me at the theatre this morning?"

He nodded.

"I'd like you to be there, my dear. Unless you've other plans."

"No." She had hoped to be released, this once. Excellent critic though she was, it wouldn't be easy for her to concentrate on things to-day. It never was, when a letter came. "I'll drive up with you, then."

The cigarette, extended by the black holder, jutted from his face like a balloon-stick. "Good. By lunch-time we shall be through with our Scene One; then we can talk it over somewhere with a salad." He looked at his watch and got up, collecting those letters that he must take to the theatre. "This morning's work will be rather important, and I'm going to give you the power of verdict."

"I hope I shan't let you down, Harrison."

"If you do, it will be a precedent. Give you ten minutes."

"I'm ready now, almost."

"It's always the almost that takes ten minutes...I'll be in the car."

As he opened the french doors she called, "Harrison?"

He turned.

"Yes, my dear?"

She stood by the other door. Between them were the flowers on the table; they saw each other over the heads of yellow roses.

"Thank you for—saying such nice things to me, that's all. You always pander to my liver at breakfast."

He took the cigarette-holder slowly from his mouth, smiling to her, a little surprised, over the roses.

"Dear Nicole, if you ever have a liver, I shall leave you entirely alone until it's gone. I know my limitations."

She opened the door; the duty was done. She had tried to make amends for all the deceit and the ugliness and the estrangement that had dwelled between them among the yellow blooms; but she knew that if she ever wanted Harrison back, she must do so much more than that.

In fewer than ten minutes she crossed the porch in her flowered tie-silk dress and white sandals; the click of her heels over the stone was loud in the early sunshine; she carried a summer straw and a French wicker bag; and there was in her walk a quickness, in her eyes a brightness; suddenly she was young at twenty-nine.

In the bag was the envelope, ripped and ragged; and it mattered so much what the letter had said.

"I don't know. See what you can make of it."

"All right. Go ahead."

Bishop focused his gaze on the stripes of the Regency curtains; along their clean perspective he selected his thoughts. Inspector Frisnay watched a sparrow that was fretting at crumbs on his austere window-sill. Between the two men the wires ran, stretched their threads across a thousand buildings, beneath a hundred streets.

"She is, I think, a little bit crass. Highly melodramatic and not frightfully intelligent. A good actress, both on and off the stage. She had a row with
Trafford on Saturday night—the fourteenth—in his
dressing-room, and she was the vociferous antag-
onist the porter heard in the hotel between midnight and one o'clock."

"Did she admit that?"

"As good as. I gave her the impression that I knew
it anyway, and she didn't correct me."

"Bishop, how the hell did you find this woman?
I rang you last Saturday and told you about a brunette who'd apparently stayed with Trafford that
night, and you said the very same woman was coming to see you that evening."

"I didn't. I said it might be she."

"Well it was. How did you get on to her?"

"Luck."

"Rot."

"As you will."

Frisnay looked daggers at the sparrow on his sill.

"All right, we'll save our time. What else happened?"

"Oh, we got talking about Trafford, and she suddenly went frightfully intuitive and built up a complete case against me. Said I'd killed the kid
because of my burning passion for an unnamed
lady—"

"Who?"

"I said an unnamed lady, please be more attentive, Freddie. Anyhow, her case against me was wildly elaborate and very funny. Much more elaborate and much less funny than the one I built up against *her*."

Frisney regarded his sparrow with sudden interest.

"Go on."

"You see, Helen Ledine was just wild about her Roy; and resented highly the intrusion of—"

Frisnay waited, squeezing his ear against the phone. After a bit he said:

"You still there?"

Bishop's eyes ran down the Regency stripes and came to rest on an ivory cigarette-box.

"Yes. Sorry, but something just struck me. Look here, Freddie, give me a break. You know from what I've just said that it might be worth putting tags on this Ledine woman. I think you might decide to do that, even if I don't say another word— which I'm not going to. But give me four days."

"To do what in?"

"Check up on her myself. Whatever I find, I'll let you know on . . . next Saturday night. If I discover anything really warm, I'll contact you even sooner."

Frisnay glowered at his sparrow.

"My dear fellow, you ought to realise that when you get on to me and hand out information I'm bound to take it up if I consider it's good."

"I realise that."

"I'm glad. You've just given me a lead that might end in a cul-de-sac or might open up the whole issue. You can't suddenly repent and ask me to forget it for four days."

"Well I am. Listen, son. With the kindest intentions I've just handed you a lead; but it suddenly occurred to me that I can do more than you, alone, on this particular line. If I haven't done anything in four days, it's all yours."

"I don't like this. It's unusual. Whenever you've turned any information my way in the past you've turned it clean and given me the all-clear. Now you want to play coy and leave me picking my nails."

"Now don't drag in irrelevant childhood habits. I'm simply acknowledging that if I'd thought things out more carefully before phoning you I'd never have phoned you at all. So you're luckier than maybe, for a start. I'm also asking you a favour, on the strength of all the other stuff I've given you in the past. Just pigeonhole what I've just said about Ledine until Saturday night. If I've turned up nothing by then, it goes over to you."

After a long time Frisnay said:

"I can't promise."

"Then you're a louse."

"I like it."

"You must."

"But I'll do my best to hold it off until Saturday.

I promise I'll do my best."

"You may do, you fickle-hearted treacherous wire-worm, your worst. And I hope it give you pimples."

Bishop dropped his phone.

Frisnay looked at his vacant window-sill; the little sparrow that had told him so much had flown.

In the room above King's Road, Bishop was furious. He had nearly, in his talk to Frisnay, implicated Nicole. He had already said too much. If Frisnay went after Ledine, she would bring Nicole into it; and Bishop tried to keep to one of his strictest rules: that he never offered to help anyone unless he could do without bringing them into the limelight. At the moment Nicole Pedley was outside its range; but if Frisnay went to Ledine...

Bishop's fingers drummed on the limed-oak desk with a militant rhythm. He had sailed too near the wind; all right—he'd put about.

He was almost certain that the inspector would take up this new lead, because the case of the missing actor was now thought to be more serious. Bishop was convinced that Trafford was dead; and it was on that premise that so many theories hinged.

He moved his hand to the telephone, but it rang as his fingers touched it. He opened the line.

"Yes?"

"Is that Mr. Bishop?"

Her low voice came clearly. He said:

"Hello, Mrs. Pedley. How are you?"

"Well, thank you. I—I haven't more than a second to talk—"

"Shoot then."

"I thought I should let you know about something. I've got an invitation from Roy to meet him for lunch to-day, at the Honey Pot."

He looked steadily at the dial of the telephone.

"That's in Gerrard Street, isn't it?"

"Yes."

"What time?"

"One o'clock."

"Good. Don't keep him waiting, will you?"

Her voice was tremulous. "I certainly won't. Shall I phone you later?"

"Please. I shall be here."

"All right—good-bye."

"Good-bye."

He cradled the receiver, and for a long time sat and gazed at it.

8_th_

MOVE

"NO!"

It echoed, the single word, across the gaping seats to the gallery; the auditorium was hollow with it. In the hush that followed, faces turned, and nobody spoke.

The call-boy sat transfixed on his crate. The carpenter went on turning his screwdriver at the back of the stage; but his hand twisted tentatively, ready to stop if it made a sound that would carry out to that awful silence. On the stage, Dincock bit his lip.

"Mr. Dincock," the voice came again. It was no longer loud; it was deathly calm; the enunciation was pedantic and over-precise. "Mr. Dincock, allow me to remind you that you have been brutally slain by one you held to be your close accomplice but a moment ago."

Again the silence came. The round, sparse-haired head made no movement in the stalls. It was poised like a rock on the dark plush of the seat, and from it there issued the stone-like consonants that were deadened only by the deceitful softness of the sibilants.

"Consider, Mr. Dincock, the implications. To find yourself stabbed must surprise you. It does: you have it in your tones. But more than that you find a traitor's blade in you. As you die you know surprise, and agony—and, most of all, an amazement amounting almost to disbelief that it should be Iago—of all people—who has done this thing."

Dincock listened, facing his producer over the footlights' unlit bulbs. Let the devil go on. Let him talk himself hoarse. This was a morning for the lot of them. Before, it was Marion; and he wondered she hadn't gone home for a bit of peace. Then it was Mathieson; but even he had taken it well enough. Now for "Mr." Dincock. Well, it was his turn.

Beside the producer, Nicole Pedley sat. She was not looking at the stage, but down at a notebook. That was nice of her, Dincock thought. She must have the hell of a time married to that pompous megaphone.

"Let us then, Mr. Dincock, hear a little of what is in the line. Help us, if you will, to imagine the feelings of this dying man as he struggles in his agony to reconcile the blade and the hand that grips it. Offer us your stupefaction, your rage, your suffering, your final disillusionment in the very moment of your death."

The voice was rich, the intonations were superb; the words were loosely chosen but their tone was all. Behind the stage the carpenter's hand had stopped; he had been forced to listen to that voice, he—thank God!—was not its victim.

"Our morning's work has not gone well, ladies and gentlemen." He looked at his watch, jerking his wrist deliberately. "In a few minutes it will be time for lunch." The boulder-like head rocked back again and the bright brown eyes focused upon Roderigo. "Mr. Dincock—and others—let us pray that what we are about to receive will be at least well earned."

The carpenter gave a sigh. The call-boy swallowed, but wasn't certain that it was all over. Nicole looked down at her notebook with her eyes narrowed and her nerves tortured under tension; because this crisis was nothing. The other, that would come in a few minutes, would be unbearable. She sat, sickened. The silence lasted another moment, and Dincock decided that he could continue, now that Pedley had played to his gallery once again.

Drawing a slow breath to ensure a steadiness of tone, Dincock said clearly:

"Thank you."

Relaxation was visible, audible, tangible. A face turned, a seat creaked, pressure lifted. Pedley said nothing more. Brockley, Ferson and Dincock resumed their places. The three others waited. Dincock began.

"O, help me here!"

"That's one of them!"

"O murderous slave! O villain!"

The dagger flashed; feet thudded on the dusty boards. Dincock fell, staring up at Ferson open-mouthed and agonised. From the stalls, Pedley watched, immobile.

"O damn'd Iago! O inhuman dog!"

The words came hollow from a dying throat and held a sob of rage, a choke of disbelief; and Dincock slumped, and was silent. The line had been delivered most superbly, but the producer stared on without even a nod to acknowledge it. Words ran on, communing with his ears.

"Kill men i' the dark! Where be these bloody thieves? How silent is this town! Ho! Murder! Murder!—What may you be? Are you of good or evil?"

"As you shall prove us, praise us."

"Signior Lodovico?"

"He, sir."

"I cry you mercy. Here's Cassio hurt by villains!"

Harrison Pedley stood up. The words were cut off. Dincock half rose and leaned on one elbow. The call-boy had left his crate and was edging about. Pedley said:

"Thank you, gentlemen. We shall be ready again at two o'clock."

The stage cleared. Ferson said something to Brockley and Brockley laughed. The carpenter began hammering now that the din wouldn't make no odds, and his mate came in through the double doors with sandwiches and a Thermos.

As Nicole got up her legs were weak. For two hours her mind had been at the mercy of a rising tension. The hands of the white-faced clock beside the stage had moved with an exquisite slowness, twisting the core of her nerves until they were as taut as the spokes of a wheel.

In her bag had lain the letter, and the few words of its message had become linked and entangled with the lines whose execution she was here to judge for Harrison. Now it was over, and the point was reached where there must come the crisis that she had feared for days; unless she ignored the letter. She could do that.

Or she could ignore Harrison.

After a good morning's work it might have been easy to plead a headache, to choose the right words and the perfect tone, to exploit his innate gentleness and rouse his sympathy. He would have excused her from the vital discussion at lunch. He valued her critical faculties for precisely their worth to his work; and their worth was great; but he would have asked her verdict later, when she had rested, if she could have approached him in easier circumstances.

But the morning's rehearsal had been much less than good; or Harrison had found fault where there was none. Everything had gone awry, and he had shown less patience than he might. He had worked harder than any on the stage, but they had striven with him, and the last scene had been a model of technique, a lyric of the uttered word. Yet his mood, placated, could not in one moment change. He had given them hell and they had given him performances that would have stilled the very breathing of a crowded house; but it would not be until the day's end that he would relax, and thank the company with the strange humility that they knew, at such rare moments, to be genuine.

Until then, let them beware of him. Let them take their warning from his quietness, his unmoving gaze, his sudden eruption of impatience that was better than the long, tenuous silences that filled the auditorium and shocked their ears.

They knew his mood, as they left the theatre for lunch; and none of them knew it so well as did his wife.

As she walked with him between the front row

and the orchestra-pit, she tried to make her decision, and as she tried, clenching her fingers in the slim white gloves, beating down the flutter in her throat, she began to panic.

There was no time; perhaps a moment or two, no longer. It was ten to one, and Harrison was taking her to the nearest restaurant where they could eat a salad and confer on the morning's work—she had agreed to that, after breakfast, over the yellow roses in the bowl. But in ten minutes, Roy would be waiting in Gerrard Street, the briefest walk from here...

"...Perhaps the hot weather, yes, I know; but in winter we have the cold weather and in autumn there's the wind—once allow these extenuations and a company will go to pieces under your gaze."

He paused, waiting for her to go first into the long passage. In normal mood his manners were excellent; in these times of vigorous ebullience they were impeccable.

"Forgive my lecturing, Nicole—this morning's display of mediocrity was at least no fault of yours. I thank God and you that we can get away for an hour and try to make sense of gibberish."

She slowed her steps beside him; and he walked on down the corridor past the dressing-rooms, his voice ahead of him, and he ahead of her. The three of them went towards the stage door, the voice, the man and the woman; and the woman nearly screamed.

"If Scene One is not finished by this evening, then it will be rehearsed into the night, rehearsed and rehearsed until the morning if needs be, rehearsed until—"

"Harrison."

It sobbed out of her but the echoes of his voice drowned the tone, freed only the word, his name. He stopped, and at the stage door turned, slightly out of breath. A shaft of sunlight was slanting into the doorway and it drowned him in its flat white glare.

"Yes, my dear?"

The clitter of her heels died as she caught up with him. "Harrison, I'm feeling—rather funny." She passed a hand over her brow, not very well because she felt too sick to pretend efficiently. "Could you let me have an hour's rest somewhere, I—"

"My dear, of course!"

He held her arm, firmly, assisting her across the pavement to the near-side of the car. "It's been a wicked day for everyone, and I'm not surprised that the reaction's setting in."

He opened the driving door and slammed it lightly after him, starting the engine. "You shall rest where it is cool and quiet. I was going to suggest Green's but it's too open to the sun. I know a better place, and just as near."

Panic was in her now, but even it was blunted

by its own despair. It was too hot to care. It was too sordid to believe. It was too French-novelette to take seriously. She sat beside her husband and he swung the wheel.

It had been difficult, sometimes, to meet Roy without letting people know, without being sorry for Harrison and afraid for herself even in her lover's arms. It had been difficult to keep alive her love for Roy when the letters had come and he had disappeared so strangely. But now it was too much.

She was within minutes of meeting her lover who had vanished and had asked her for money in his first brief note; and such a lover as this was dreaming on, while her husband drove her, asking gently:

"Shall we open the roof, my dear?"

Her head lifted; her eyes opened wider.

"Please."

He used his left hand, sliding back the roof-panel with a jerk. They turned into Gerrard Street. As he parked the car she looked up, coming to the surface of a quasi-coma that developed to deaden her nerves. Her eyes focused on the painted board that hung above the windows. It was a pretty place with geraniums and bottle-glass panes and a quaint door the shape of a bee-hive.

"In here," Harrison said gently, "we can shed our hot humours. Salad . . . and ice . . . and a shaded corner. It's never crowded."

She got out of the Lea-Francis, knowing that it

was too late now to try even to think. She was almost glad that by sheer chance he had selected the Honey Pot—by chance and perhaps her own stupidity. She knew they would have gone, as usual, to Green's; but this place was smaller and more shaded, and half below street-level and therefore cool. She had asked to come here, in a way. Her escort, a man whose manners were a knight's, had obeyed her unthinking whim.

The situation sent a stupid lightness through her head as she crossed the pavement and passed under the awning with Harrison; it was too contrived, too extravagant for any tragi-comedy, yet it was real, and she was part of it.

As she walked between the great stone bowls of pink azaleas and felt the coolness of the downward steps, she knew that she had made the decision. She had had to ignore Roy, or Harrison. She was lunching with her husband and not her lover. It had been quite simple. She could never have persuaded Harrison to leave her even for an hour: he was filled with the morning's problems and the problems that would come; he must talk to someone, take the rehearsal to pieces line by line to unearth imperfection. And she was his partner, his critic, his judge. She could not have done anything other than this, even if the heat and the oppressive atmosphere of the rehearsal had left her wits less jaded.

They reached the base of the steps and were among light oak panelling, flowers and silver, white shirt fronts and bowing smiles, and the small glass bulbs of percolators over blue buds of flame. Nicole said:

"Please, not too much of anything," and turned away to the cloakroom. The surface of the mirrored table was hard so that her writing was spidery, and not steady. A sheen of perspiration was on her hand. The attendant, a plump cheerful woman with a little harsh laugh, kept up a discussion about the hot weather and how cool it was down here.

"Of course, it's being a basement, so to speak. The sun jus' can't get down here, not down all those steps."

She laughed expansively.

It's quite impossible, so sorry.

"But then we get it both ways. In the winter there's the boilers next door, so we're as hot as we like. A bit hotter at times!"

She laughed comfortably about her boilers.

To-morrow? Or will you phone? Take care.

"I suppose it's killing up in the street? I always think of my husband days like this. Works in the open—master-roadman—he gets brown as a choc'late!"

She laughed sympathetically about her husband.

Au revoir.

The pencil rested. It dropped into the bottom of

the bag-pocket and she took out her lipstick, hurrying now. Then she thanked the woman and turned left outside the screened door. The desk was not in sight of the majority of tables. It didn't matter if he noticed. She could use some excuse.

"Has a Mr. Trafford booked a table for one o'clock?"

The thick finger ran down the columns and stopped.

"Yes, Madam."

She stopped him in time. "No-no, I'm not with him. But when he arrives, please let him have this."

"Certainly, Madam."

He bowed over the tiny folded slip before it went into the trellis-ribbon board behind him. She turned away, and when she was guided to Harrison's table she knew that he could not have seen her at the desk.

"Sorry to have been so long."

He sat down again. "You've been very quick—but still too long."

She smiled to him, because if she didn't smile about this situation she would sicken with it. Her chair faced the main room; she would see everyone coming in.

"I've ordered Dubonnet," Harrison said.

"Lovely."

Strange that Roy should still be using his real name. He was thought to be missing, unaccountably.

"You are guilty, my dear, of a secret genius. For days we've sat in the sun at Green's, and all the time there was this shady dug-out round the corner."

"But this was your suggestion."

"You wanted somewhere cool, and I remembered it. We must repair hither upon days cursed with a temperature in excess of seventy-five. Agreed?"

"Agreed."

To-morrow? No...already the note should be amended. To-day was to be the first of a hellish series. He would bring her here to-morrow, because to-morrow would be as warm. It had just been agreed. Could she do nothing right, even by luck?

"Are you feeling less wobbly?" he asked gently.

She nodded.

"Much. I'm sorry I wilted—it really was rather a powerful morning."

Two people came round the corner where the tiny fountain splashed in its Japanese garden. A man and a woman. When Roy came in, would they remember the note?

"That was possibly my fault, in the main. I may have been supercritical; but there was no excuse for Dincock."

And if they remembered the note, and he read it, would he cancel the table and leave?

"He may have felt the heat. I can't be the only one. And he gave you all you asked for, just before we packed up."

Harrison shrugged with his hands.

"To a less gory afternoon," he said as she lifted her *apéritif.*

Or would he decide to show himself, impetuously? Roy was good at passionate impulses. If he came to this table, everything would crash. Harrison scarcely knew him, but he had heard of the disappearance; most people in the theatre had heard.

"Now I must pop the vital question, Nicole. Are we to go on to the end of the scene after lunch? Or begin again and make a night of it?"

His eyes were serious; he had been half-afraid to ask her this. So much would depend on this day's work, more perhaps than upon others. In a few nights they would open. By then it must be perfect, it must be malleable by the experience of the first two or three performances; then it would settle and cohere.

Begin again? Night of it? She had caught the words as they had slipped past her, ousted by her thoughts. Now she played them back and heard their sense, guessing their lost context.

She said: "No, Harrison. It was too good. We had force and we had polish coming up very clearly. Peter's off colour for some reason but if you don't

137

flay him too badly this afternoon I think he'll go well."

Tall figures were moving across the surface of her Dubonnet and she glanced up. Four people were coming down the middle of the room, talking too loudly. One of them was the mad Francesca woman from *Whipped Cream*. She was talking very loudly and happily about Francesca and *Whipped Cream*. It was folding in a week and she was gaily desperate.

"What about Dincock?"

The four sat down with a flourish, seeming to push the surrounding tables aside, seeming to press away the background murmur and raise a great pillar of Babel for all to hear who cared, or could not help it.

"He was off colour too, and anyway his scene's finished. I should rest him for a day and we'll have a grand-slam."

"Harrison, if Roy comes up and talks to us there's going to be murder. You won't worry about Dincock or opening-night. Darling you'll get so hurt and I'm afraid of that."

"Very well, we'll just see how we can go on. I agree that if we go back over the first part we'll be putting everyone in the wrongest mood."

Their salad came. It had everything nice, was more colourful than the tiny fountain in its Japanese garden. Someone came in, alone, a woman, nobody Nicole knew.

The four people in the middle of the room laughed in unison, frightfully pleased with themselves, frantically gay. Their waiter wore a fixed smile.

"I'm sorry," Nicole said, "I haven't given you a very brilliant summing-up. Will you make it a straight questionnaire?"

He touched her hand with his finger-tips. His mood had passed more quickly than usual, perhaps in deference to her heat-wave *malaise*.

"We'll leave it as it stands, my dear. Despite the heady weather you've given me back all the confidence I felt in the theatre. I'm very grateful."

"You're very sweet to me. Too forgiving."

Francesca shrieked from the middle table, "And that was simply the very *end* ... I told him where to go and my *dears* he simply *went*. And none more staggered than I!"

"When the time comes," Harrison said quietly, "when I can't forgive you anything, then I shall have stopped loving you, so it won't matter to you any more. That thing yonder," he went on broodingly, "that bears a human form, that monument of all that is gross in female shape, that bag of wind, that belly-gust ... should be reminded that God gave to us the gift of tongue and the benison of words ... Her head is empty and her mouth is full, her breath is burdened with such spate of frenzied gibberish that would a drunken monkey put to instant shame ..."

"The metre slipped in parts," she smiled carefully, "but on the whole a fair comment."

"Thank you."

He began his salad.

Harrison, you should have a different wife, a plain wife who doesn't crave physical, animal things, a tall woman with great poise and a better appreciation of what you are, of what you feel. If you find me out I'll be a stone, blunting you. When I married I was blinded by your brilliant mind, I forgot bodies and sensual looks; and now it's too late to remember them without risking all of the other thing, the spirit. If we could go back...

"You, my dear, or the Dubonnet, have given me a sense of sudden well-being that even that fleshy megaphone can't destroy."

She found the knife and fork in her hands, and began moving them, remembering. "I'm glad, Harrison."

"I brought you here to conduct a full-scale inquest on a foul morning's work, and you dismissed my fears in a few words and left me released from doubt. I think our play will be a very good play. I feel that."

She watched him for an instant. A tenderness grew in her as she saw the calm face and the gentle eyes, the eagerness in his voice when he spoke of his play; like a plump schoolboy remembering his tuck-box back in the dormitory.

"I feel it too," she said. "It's going to be a truly memorable first night."

It meant nothing, this sense of confidence, of well-being. By the first night he would be hollow with nerves, prey to the worst despair until the curtain rose. Between now and then he would give the company heaven and give them hell; in the end he would give them a play of value that would equal exactly the cost.

A reflection glided across her glass and for the hundredth time she glanced upwards, and this time did not look down, relieved. Fifteen minutes had been arced away on the clock-face above the fountain, and now a man was coming in, alone.

For a moment he looked round, his eyes travelling with an easy glance until he saw her at the corner table. Then he came across.

Harrison said, "Tell me what you're going to wear, on the first night. Describe in perfect detail."

Her eyes were expressionless until the man was near; and then, seeing that he was slightly smiling, she took his unspoken lead, and acknowledged him. Harrison was looking up, following her gaze.

"Well, well—Mrs. Pedley. How are you?"

She gave him her hand lightly as Pedley stood up.

"How nice to see you again...Harrison, this is a friend of mine—Mr. Bishop. Mr. Bishop, my husband..."

The two men looked at each other.

9th
MOVE

"YOU BELIEVE TRAFFORD will turn up at the Honey Pot?"

Bishop shrugged, picking up his gloves by the door.

"Can't say. It's highly odd. We'll see."

"Take care, Hugo."

He left her with a pained expression, closing the door softly. Miss Gorringe relaxed. She knew his mood: for half an hour he had been restless, over-frivolous in his remarks, as if he were pleased with himself but wasn't certain why.

Something was off his mind for a while. Something to do with the Nicole Pedley case had broken, and he was alert to that. He had told Vera Gorringe nothing, but she knew he would choose the moment. This was not the first time she had found herself standing-by when a case showed all the signs of breaking. It was always a little unnerving, like waiting for the doctor to come. And it was sometimes worse afterwards: a few months ago when he had been working on a tricky problem in drug trafficking, he had put his finger on exactly the right spot—it had happened to be a trigger—and the case had closed the same day. In the evening, Miss Gorringe had located him fifty feet beneath the pavements of Leicester Square in an all-hour strictly-under-your-hat spirits bar with a blonde gin-sprite on his arm and a paper hat on his head and a bullet still lodged in the heel of his shoe. He had been singing snatches of *Il Trovatore* to the tune of *Tiger Rag*.

Vera Gorringe smiled wistfully at her filing-cabinet, remembering the episode, and other episodes, until she reached the memorable day when she had seen the advertisement, and had answered it. The phrasing had been typical.

> **Wanted**: a Factotum of Neuter Gender, Irreligious and Non-political, who will Factote Invisibly and Inaudibly and will neither Bath too Little nor Drink too Much nor Otherwise Offend.

Miss Vera J. Gorringe, M.A. (Oxon), had looked round her study with critical appraisal, compared it with a hermit's cave and found the contrast slight, and wrote her reply to the address in Chelsea:

I am far from neuter even at my age, my religion is my own business, politically my views are philosophical, I am too large to factote invisibly, too heavy to be inaudible, I bath daily and require a full hour regardless of competitors for the amenities, I drink when extremely happy, extremely depressed or simply thirsty, and any offence given would depend upon the sense of humour of the recipient. Your advertisement reveals a kind of childlike disposition that might prove refreshing after years of celibate erudition, and so I apply for the post. Please submit references and state number of wives.

Two weeks later she had been interviewed, invited to have her private room in the flat redecorated to her own taste, and there installed. Since then she had given her notice twice a month. It had never been accepted.

"Your Highness," she said softly to Chu Yi-Hsin, "Mr. Bishop is working up to one of his periodical orgies of dire skull-duggery. We must be on our guard."

The Princess Chu Yi-Hsin observed her with a tranquil gaze, and turned a strange little sound in her throat. She knew nothing of the words, but acknowledged that the person she liked so well was addressing her in a gentle voice.

At twenty minutes to one the venerable Rolls-Royce drew with quiet dignity into the kerbside. From its position near the corner of a smaller road off Gerrard Street, Bishop could survey the entrance of the Honey Pot.

At a little before the hour he noted the grey Lea-Francis saloon that parked not far off, and saw Mr. and Mrs. Pedley enter the bee-hive doorway. Twice he checked the photograph of Trafford that he had obtained from the theatre, but its original did not appear. At one-fifteen he left the car and went into the Honey Pot. He decided to do this out of hand. The telephone call from Nicole had interested him, because he had believed Trafford to be dead. If he were alive, and had made this appointment with her, why had he come into the open after taking such careful steps to remain hidden? If he were not alive, and someone else had made this appointment, why was *he* coming into the open? If he had made the appointment with no intention of keeping it, what was his purpose?

Most interesting of all: why had Nicole brought her husband here, to this place, at this time?

In pursuit of the answers to these curious points, Bishop crossed the road and went down the cool stone steps. The miniature fountain played silverly in the Japanese garden. The head-waiter was anxious to select him a table. In this he was discouraged, and left his guest to greet his two friends in the corner.

After the introduction Pedley said:

"Won't you join us?"

"I feel I shouldn't."

Pedley sat down.

"Oh, come! Nicole sees so little of her friends these days. Work has reached that pitch—" he nodded to the waiter—"please yes, another chair."

In a profound voice one of the party of four in the middle of the room said, "He reminds me ... *so* much ... of someone. Now who?"

Francesca said, "Leslie Howard, darling."

"But of course! Poor *dear* Leslie—but you're so right!"

Bishop turned his newly offered chair a few inches to the left, so that its back faced the middle of the room.

"Work," he said, "must certainly have reached that pitch. But it's going magnificently."

Pedley raised his brows.

"A gracious tribute to mere reputation, sir?"

"Not entirely. I'm afraid I slipped through the defences of the Parthenon last Sunday and sat in the most shadowed seat I could find."

"During rehearsals?" Nicole asked softly.

"Yes. I do apologise, but it was worth the risk of being ejected. Was it inexcusable?"

"Your illicit presence, certainly," said Pedley, "but your imminent criticism, never. Unless of course it's favourable."

"Completely. I savoured every moment."

"Particularly my lecturing of young Ferson, no doubt."

"That was classic, Mr. Pedley."

"Ferson didn't think so, Mr. Bishop." A gentle rumble of humour escaped him. "Er—would you care to start with our wine, or—?"

"Thanks, but I lunched early."

"Coffee, then, and a liqueur."

"I mustn't disturb you—"

"We shan't be long. We'll see the curtain together with peach brandy. Tell me, Mr. Bishop, what shall Nicole wear at the theatre, on our first night? We were discussing it when you arrived so happily."

Bishop glanced at her.

"Surely it's quite unimportant," he said gently.

"Why, thank you," said Pedley. He pressed her hand affectionately. "The subject is only slightly more deserving than the compliment, but that lifts achievement to the sublime."

He signalled their waiter. "An ice, my dear?"

"I don't think so."

"Coffee, then, and your colleague of the cellar."

"M'sieur."

"You will, of course, be with us on the first night, Mr. Bishop?"

"I've had two seats booked for some time."

"Pity, I could have had the pleasure of presenting you with them. Meanwhile—" he glanced up. "Some Marie Brizard, if you please—peach brandy. Suit you, Mr. Bishop? Good." He offered his cigar-case. "Meanwhile I hope that when you have a moment to drop in during rehearsals again you'll mention my name at the stage-door, and thus leave your conscience in the cloakroom."

"Many thanks, I'll do that."

"This afternoon, perhaps?"

"Much as I should like to, no. I've an auction at three, at Waring's."

"Ah. Glass?"

"Mainly ivory. Chess-pieces are what I'm looking for especially."

Pedley lowered his cigar and his round face puckered into eagerness. "You play? How nice to discover that. We must have a game. When?"

Nicole raised her liqueur, her green eyes away from either face. Life was droll. She had arranged to sit here with Roy, but Roy had not come and Harrison had, together with the strange Mr. Bishop. There was a mischief in the sun's heat to-day; something quite unknown had taken control of her affairs.

"At the moment you are busier than I," Bishop

said. "I'll leave the time to you."

Pedley spread his hands. "This evening, then. Is it possible?"

"I've no plans—"

"Excellent! Come to dinner, and we'll wage a tournament by sunset, on the lawn. Can you think in the open air?"

"Better than indoors."

"Nicole, my dear—?"

"Of course, I'll ring Maria—though it'll be something cold, Hugo. We haven't asked for cooking since the heatwave started."

"Anything cold will be delicious. I find I can go two days in this heat on a glass of orange-juice and a lettuce."

And still he ignored the slow questioning of her eyes.

She said, "Shall we be late at the theatre, Harrison?"

"I doubt it, my dear. Mr. Bishop, perhaps you'll meet us there, and we can all drive to Hampstead?"

"Very well, what time?"

"Shall we say six?"

"Perfect. I shall walk boldly through the stage door."

"Of course—in future. If you are free before six, we might have the pleasure of seeing you at the tail-end of rehearsal."

"I shall certainly try."

Pedley nodded, leaving his eyes for a moment on the lean chiselled face of his wife's friend. Bishop seemed to interest him considerably. For a moment more he gazed, his eyes appraising the features and perhaps trying to deduce from their character that of the man; then Bishop turned his head, and looked back at Pedley.

It was one of those sudden instances when something has to be said to break the silent surveillance. Pedley asked:

"How is Helen?"

The question was surprising and irrelevant.

"As Helen always is," Bishop said. Nicole was looking at him over her cigarette. The wide green eyes were grave and puzzled, and a little afraid of something. "Throwing herself into things with her usual *élan*."

Pedley smiled indulgently.

"A strange woman. She has a mind like a kaleidoscope."

"Perfect simile," nodded Bishop. "Present her with one commonplace subject and it becomes a riotous pattern of the most complex design. But a likeable personality."

He tried to think out the connection, but there were so many links, so many combinations: he had seen Helen Ledine last Saturday night—four nights ago. Since then she must have mentioned him to Pedley. Or must have talked to Nicole, who had

talked to Pedley. Or there must be a new link—
Helen: a Friend: Nicole (Friend common to both):
Pedley. But it had begun with Helen, however it
had reached him. Helen had told someone that she
had been at his flat on Saturday night.

That might be vitally significant, or simply a common instance of a name being passed around during innocent conversation.

Nicole said, "She must be even more kaleido-
scopic than usual to-day." She was talking directly
to Bishop. "Harrison has chosen her for the lead in
Autumn Gold."

"I haven't heard about that. I mean the play."

"It's something rather special. A new playwright,
a new subject."

"More than special, then. Unique."

Pedley grunted a laugh. "You sound like a sour
critic, Mr. Bishop."

"I didn't mean to. But we can do with a new
subject on the London stage."

"I agree, I agree. It's refreshing. That is why I
decided to risk giving Helen the plum. She has
never played the lead before in the West End. Nicole is of the opinion that the risk is too great; or
that Helen is too little in stature." He raised his
brows, questioning Bishop.

"I'm not qualified to judge. I've only seen her
once or twice."

"But she left some impression—good or bad."

"Neither, I think."

"Worse than bad? Indifferent?"

"This is ground I should keep off. If Helen Ledine has been selected—after what must have been a very careful search—to play the lead in a special Harrison Pedley production, then the most I can say is that her stature has risen in my estimation."

"I just hope," Nicole said, "that we're not making a mistake. They can be costly at the box-office."

"We shall see," Pedley smiled easily. "Meanwhile—" he looked up to the clock on the wall.

"Meanwhile I'm holding up rehearsals," Bishop said.

As they left their table, something of Nicole's tension returned. Roy had not come; or, if he had come, he had seen Harrison with her, and had gone. But he might be waiting somewhere else, outside here or at the theatre. He would not have agreed to see her without first deciding that it was important that they should meet; Roy would not be lightly put off.

He was not outside; or, if he was, he did not show himself. Pedley slid behind the wheel of his car. Bishop held the door open for Nicole on the other side. Softly she murmured as she thanked him, "Why did you come?"

"Just in case," he smiled down, and closed her door.

Pedley pressed the starter. "We shall expect you at the theatre, Mr. Bishop—at six or earlier."

"I shall look forward to that."

He stood away, and watched the saloon as it reached the first corner and turned from sight. Within ten minutes he was moving down Shaftesbury Avenue in the grey Rolls-Royce. As he reached the Circus and swung right into Piccadilly, a man walked down Gerrard Street and went into the Honey Pot. Most of the people had gone. At the desk he asked if there were a message for a Mr. Trafford, and he was handed the folded slip of paper from the trellis-ribbon board.

He put it, still folded and unread, into his pocketbook, and climbed the steps, and passed between the flower-bowls, and came to the sunlit street.

10th

MOVE

 "I DO APOLOGISE, but I'm sure you understand."

The A.S.M. came up, script open in his hand. People were crowded in the wings; behind, hammering was nervous and hurried. Mathieson was growling his lines down left.

"Of course."

Nicole looked at Bishop, steadily.

"Leave the phrase as it stands," Pedley said, "and the gesture can be exaggerated." The A.S.M. looked very worried. "If they don't get it then, they can put what construction on it they please. Damn it, we're not playing to cretins!"

A wave of purple brocade washed down the canvas as the rolled material fell; hands held the top

154

edge; a face stood back. "Magnifico! Keep it there a moment!"

The A.S.M. shrugged and went off, the script drooping in his hand. Somewhere backstage Desdemona laughed; she had a free and rather dirty laugh and it sent others off for no reason. Pedley said:

"The mood is right. I could work them till morning if I chose. My dear—"

"Don't worry about us, Harrison. I'll leave the car for you—Hugo can take me in his."

"Mr. *Pedley*, sir!"

A man swung monkeylike on a rope, peering down at the knot of people. Electric cable was round his shoulders like surplus from a spider's spinneret.

"That would be most helpful. Thank you, Mr. Bishop."

Nicole said as she turned away, "Phone as soon as you leave here, and I'll tell Maria."

"I will, I will—"

"Shall I drop this one here, Mr. Pedley?"

"Forgive me, please—"

Bishop waved a sympathetic hand and followed Nicole along the row of seats. The carpenter's mate brought a hammer down with the definitiveness of a door slammed upon an argument.

Her heels tapped delicately along the stone passage.

"Do you really mind?" her voice floated back to him. "I don't play chess."

"I'd like to talk."

"And I." She sounded a little hopeless.

Outside he opened the near-door of the vintage Rolls. "Take yourself seriously, it's like climbing into a howdah."

"It is, rather. Tricky for shins."

The engine began whispering like a wraith disturbed; images of the buildings flickered along the grey cellulose; they turned round Cambridge Circus.

Neither spoke again until they reached Hampstead Road. It was gone six, but the plane trees were motionless and sun-bemused, and buses were dusty.

"Harrison was enjoying himself," Bishop said.

"Immensely. It's often like that. A hellish morning, a wonderful afternoon. He's rather brilliant, isn't he?"

"Very."

She didn't try to keep it back any longer.

"Have you found anything, Hugo?"

He studied the smooth grey surface of the road. She added, "Do you mind my calling you that?"

"Much more cosy. No, I don't believe I've found anything. A lot of queer inconsistencies, a lot of paradoxes, a lot of oddness. Tell me why you rang me this morning and pretended Trafford had made an—?"

"I wasn't pretending." She watched him steadily, the green eyes like an indignant child's. She looked to him very lovely, watching his face so solemnly and hurtly. "You trust me scarcely at all, do you?"

"These the gates?"

Her small head turned quickly as though she had forgotten they were not driving on for ever. "Oh, yes. They should be open."

"They are."

The tyres fretted over the gravel, selecting and tossing aside small stones; against the Georgian porch the car posed to a halt with a smooth flourish whose essence was the absence of mechanical effort.

"You live in a lovely house, Nicole." He stayed with his hands hanging on the wheel, reflectively. "What a pity that with such a lovely house and a brilliant husband there must be . . . all this business."

So softly that he scarcely heard she murmured, "Yes."

"Of course there should be a plain woman here, in your place. Dignified and placid, ministrative and self-effacing."

"Am I none of those things?"

She, too, did not want to get out of the car. She gazed at the house, and there was no love of it in her eyes.

"You are not plain," he said. "With your beauty,

dignity in its true sense would be incongruous. You are not placid, simply because it isn't your temperament. What else did I say the woman must possess?"

"She must be ministrative, you said."

"Obviously you're that: perhaps over-so, even considering Harrison's need of practical devotion."

The sun came down over the chimneys and sent their shadows sprawling across the lawn. On this, the east wall, ivy swarmed darkly, be-flowing the white window-frames and tidings to the eaves, as if the shadow that the sun had cast was not enough. A frailty was lacing the air, here among the roses and aubretia-beds; it was prelude to twilight, and birds called thinly.

"And the last?" she murmured. "Self-effacement?"

"I think you have that gift."

"But it's a gift, and not my nature."

"Perhaps. For another sixpense I'll tell you if you should avoid strangers this month, or should wear green—"

"Your little analysis didn't sound like that. It was rather good. I was thinking only to-day that poor Harrison should have married someone like you say. I'm too much of a slut."

"Too vital, if you will."

The leather of the seat creaked as she relaxed, closing her eyes for a moment. "I feel far from vital,

Hugo. Drained—emptied—even of anxiety."

"The heat."

"Partly."

He looked down at her face. Her lashes curved up from the closed lids like dark feathers; her lips were calm, and were sculptured with firm perfection above the clear line of her chin; her brow was filmed with the silver down of moisture. From the roof of the car, heat fell, eddying.

"In here," he said quietly, "it's very limp-making."

Her eyes did not open at once. "I wonder why," she murmured, "I can relax so well in your company, and why I call you Hugo so soon. You've done nothing for me that has helped; I don't even know you've been trying."

Her legs were drawn up against the seat-front, and her sandals were very small; her bare arms were lying together with her hands clasped loosely. She looked like a child who knew that it could sleep now, and not be afraid any more of the things outside the door.

Softly she said, "But there's an ease that I feel, like a kindly drug as if I trust you with things that not even a superman could deal with even if he wanted to. Is it very dangerous for me, do you think?"

Gently he opened his door, and got out, and strolled round to the other side, looking down at her again through the lowered window.

"It sounds rather nice," he said, "not dangerous at all."

"Your voice is incredibly hypnotic."

He let his eyes linger pleasurably on her small, warm face and the curled repose of the young body, high of breast and slim of waist under the flimsy dress; then he said quietly, "Most people's voices are hypnotic when you shut your eyes. What is more hypnotic is the heat. If you stay there another five minutes you'll doze off entirely."

Her eyes were a little startled as they opened, and she struggled up hastily.

"Oh, lor', what a hostess I'm being!"

"Careful—there's a long drop. This isn't your own opulent-looking wheeled *chaise-longue*."

She smiled up at him, sliding her wicker bag from the dashboard pocket. "Please overlook me. We ought to be viewing the kitchen-garden by this time—you are fond of kitchen-gardens, Mr. Bishop?"

"Ecstatically, but of course I haven't one myself."

"Oh, it means a lot of hard work and anxiety— the birds do *so* much damage, you know—"

"They don't seem to have, here. It looks charming."

"Oh, just a patch—one's own humble plot—"

She broke off the badinage abruptly, for they were walking on to the porch. The porch was quite in shadow, and chill rose from the heavy stone flags.

"Hugo—"

"Yes?"

"I know why I felt so snug with you in the car."

Her voice was soft still, yet there was a hint of shrillness in her throat. "It was like the last five minutes in bed, before having to get up and bath and do teeth and hair and things. I never like getting up." She tilted her head, looking at the old wrought-metal lamp, and the great white door with its ponderous knocker. "I haven't liked coming in here, either. For a long time."

Seriously he said, "That's quite natural. There's a lot of tension, in there. Pity, and subterfuge."

"Yes, I know. It's just that."

He was watching her face, intently, as they stood on the shadowed porch. He saw a mind near breaking-point.

She said, "Sometimes it seems more than that. As if there's something hideous, something—"

"Yes, isn't it strange?" He pressed her arm, going over the stone paving to the door. "Whenever we have something on our minds that's very harassing but perfectly natural we begin to feel nameless influences, begin to exaggerate. We wake with a slight earache and think of mastoids. There's only one cure and that's a neat slug."

She laughed breathlessly, opening the heavy door.

"First you have to drive me out of your car and then you have to ask outright for a drink. I don't feel you'll come here again."

"Whenever you ask me to, Nicole."

She turned in the hall, brushing back her dark hair with spread fingers.

"You mean if I get the jim-jams again I can ring you up at short notice?"

"Something like that."

"Bless you. I've always wanted an uncle."

She moved like a flash of memory to the stairs, turning again, standing very still and very flower-bright in her tie-silk dress against the dark timber of the banisters. "I'll ask Janet to let us have something cool on the little lawn at the side. There's sun there."

"Let me fix that."

"You want to prowl?"

"Other people's houses are best explored alone. You can look at the most valuable picture in the room and enjoy it without having to say—Oh, what a magnificent—er—erm—Matisse, isn't it? Oh, Dali, of *course*."

"Then go and enjoy yourself. Through there, and through the glass door. Drinks in the cabinet by the window. Gin-orange for me."

He opened the drawing-room door and saw her turn again on the stairs. She called lightly, "They're all van Gogh, anyway."

He went into the room and felt its coolness, and soft welcome. There was nothing hideous in here, nothing unnameable. This evening, if Pedley came in time for the cold dinner, there would be tension, and pity, and subterfuge; because two of them knew and one of them didn't, and it must remain like that.

They talked in low tones, because the air was calm and there were windows open above them, and Janet was in the house with Maria the cook. A letter was in his hands.

"By this morning's post?"

"Yes. I hope it makes you trust me a little more."

He didn't smile. "That was a false impression. It had occurred to me, between lunch and this evening, that you'd had a reason for bringing me to the Honey Pot by telling me on the phone that Trafford was to be there."

"A reason I would explain later?"

"Yes."

"Now you can see it was genuine. And I wouldn't necessarily have expected you to come along, even if I said he'd be there."

"Then you should know that—though it isn't apparent that I've tried to help you—I'm interested enough to have come along very definitely. Between last Friday morning, when we met, and to-day, I've spent quite a bit of time looking round. I've tried to locate Trafford—"

"Yes?"

She had interrupted swiftly, involuntarily. He shook his head. "I don't come anywhere near him."

She relaxed, laying her head against the canvas of the deck-chair. She looked cooler in a taffeta sheerline.

"Roy," she murmured, "is becoming an obsession to me." He read again the few words of the letter while she talked. "I must break it. He's lost substance since two weeks ago when I saw him last, yet he's grown more significant. He follows me about in my mind, and never lets me think of other things, other people."

The sun glared, reddening in the west, flushing the plain white paper of the letter. "That's because he hasn't vanished beyond recall, Hugo. He's not far away. He sends these letters, reminding me that even by chance I might meet him in the street, in a restaurant."

My sweet,

All right, if you must. At the Honey Pot in Gerrard Street, one o'clock to-day. I'll book a corner table. I wouldn't risk showing myself for anyone else in the world, so believe me—

I love you.

"I think what I feel for him is sustained now by curiosity, by the readiness to pity him. Might he be ill?"

Bishop folded the letter slowly and said, "No."

"Might he have had an accident?" Her head was forward again; she watched him appealingly. "I mean if something awful—something crippling—"

"No," he said. He gave her the letter. "Nicole, if Trafford had met with an accident that would have made him in any way physically abnormal, he would have sent for you. It would have served his ego magnificently. He would have revelled in the pathos, the ironic tragedy."

She didn't look away, but nodded slowly.

"That took a lot of telling me, I know. But it's right. It would have been like that, yes. An accident, then, affecting him in any way not physically but mentally?"

"No." He finished his tomato-juice and set the glass carefully on the wicker table. "Sorry to keep saying 'No' so firmly, but although I haven't found him I've come to know him, since Friday. He is not likeable. Your love for him—may I say this? Your purely physiological response to his undoubted magnetism—is based upon nothing more than contrast."

"With Harrison?"

"Of course. Harrison is middle-aged; Roy is very young. Your husband is little less than a genius in his work, and an established success; the boy is a moderate actor, is struggling for recognition. Harrison is wealthy, Roy in debt; the one affectionate, the other passionate. And, if you will permit me, your lawful partner is in your house; your lover is attainable only through a forbidden gate. Very trite, and very unoriginal, but so damnably essential to your obsession."

He filled his pipe from the pouch, trying to find among the yellow strands the words he wanted. They came: "If it is at all possible, Nicole, I should forget Trafford entirely. See him as a mere obsession; build up all the things that make you love him, and then knock them spinning until you haven't the heart or the strength to build them again."

She gave a queer little flutter of a laugh and her eyes were wide. "Is Roy dead, Hugo?"

"That's up to you."

"Really dead, I mean? Do you really know?"

He shook his head, pulling the zip of the pouch with a jerk. "I don't know. Try to think of him that way. Better your heart break than your spirit. It's the doubt that's riding you. Throw it; I'll help."

After a thrush had crossed the lawn and had plunged to the roses she said, "You're so much kinder to me than I deserve." A tremor unsteadied her voice.

"I agree." His match rasped. "Much kinder. I should feel simply an impatience with you. A fine woman is going through sheer hell for the sake of a boy who has never given her more than relief from frustration; and his price was not high. He's left you and demands money, and when he writes you a brief, reluctant and patently self-sacrificing note agreeing to favour you with an hour of his time for lunch, you torture yourself mercilessly trying to keep the appointment against Harrison's unwitting opposition. And worst of all you're torn with pity—for Harrison and for yourself; and wonder why you can't come into this house without feeling morbid and miserable."

He dropped the match-end, squinting through the smoke and seeing Pedley at the table to-day, talking of his play, adoring his young wife, sitting at a corner table—one o'clock at the Honey Pot, a cuckold unawares.

"Why don't I see all that for myself?" she breathed.

"You stand too close. You're caught up. In a year from now you'll look back and wonder how you kept your sanity—or came to lose it."

She gazed for minutes into the cloud of cedar-boughs that canopied the lawn; and when she spoke she made no reference to what had gone before.

"Are you—going to go on trying to find Roy?"

He nodded. "For a little while."

"And then?"

"And then when I've found him I shall do all I can to make him leave the country; or certainly London."

"For my sake?"

"And Harrison's. You might not stay with Harrison even when Trafford has gone; but you might at least leave him for someone worth the break. Trafford is not. Even you admit as much."

"Ye-es. And if you don't find him—when will you stop looking?"

"In four days. On Saturday night."

"Why then?"

"I've given myself that time. It'll be enough, I believe."

"Hugo, you must have theories. If you had to back your guess—where would you say Roy was?"

He thought before answering, thought deeply and discarded several replies before selecting the only one that was possible. It would be unfair to say that he believed Trafford to be dead: he had no slightest evidence of that; besides, had it been Trafford who had made to-day's appointment with her? If not Trafford, what possible purpose could anyone else have had? If these blackmailing notes were not from Trafford, they were from someone unnamed, someone who would never deliberately show himself to Nicole. If the unknown had made that appointment, he had never intended to keep it: because if he showed himself his game would break down. Then why make it? To suggest to Nicole that Trafford was still alive and in London? If that were the purpose it would be without point, because Trafford had not turned up; and the suggestion of his failure was that he was not alive, or not in London; that these letters might be from someone else.

As Bishop prepared his answer he felt that the whole solution to the matter pivoted upon this point: why had Trafford made the date and not kept it? If it were an impostor, why make the date at all?

"I think," he said slowly, "that the question of where he is might be less important than the question of will he remain there, concealed. And I think that the answer is that he will never come into the open again. Not, certainly, in London."

"You mean you don't believe I shall see him again."

"I mean that."

"Because he is dead?"

"That is a possibility."

"Or because when you find him you're going to send him away, out of the country."

"That also is a possibility."

"How would you do that?"

"I would threaten him with five years' imprisonment."

Her voice was deathly calm. "You would need me as a witness."

He matched her voice. "No, I shouldn't want to involve you directly. But Harrison signed the first cheque. The cheque will have been endorsed."

"That would mean telling Harrison."

"Yes."

"Would you do that?"

"No. I would ask you to do that."

"But you know I wouldn't ever."

"Not directly, no. But if you don't forget Trafford, if you don't stop trying to see him, if you don't give him up for dead or exiled, you'll have to tell Harrison before long. By asking him for a cheque too many, or one too large; by rousing his suspicion when you keep engagements with Trafford or by the most likely method of all: the final breakdown of your nerves. That's coming, Nicole, but it won't happen if there's anything I can do to stop it. There is much I can do—and much of it will be against your own opposition. But you're at this moment exposing yourself to such a living hell that even you will see sense if only I can show it to you clearly."

"I'm not being very intelligent, am I?" she said bitterly.

"You can't hope to be. You're at the mercy of your emotions."

"And my emotions aren't very adult."

"A little too demanding of you."

"Altogether I wonder why you try so hard to help me. I'm only a cheap chit in a mess."

"May I?" He stood up, and took her empty glass. "Same again?"

Her breathing slowed, and she smiled, ashamed.

"Sorry. I forgot the cure—a neat slug."

"Or two," he murmured as he left her. "One is not powerful enough to overcome heavy lecturing from an impudent guest."

While she heard the faint click of glass from the loggia she closed her eyes and felt the sudden shock of uneasiness that had waited until now. Now that Hugo was not talking to her the lawn was empty, and the evening was aloof, running its own life from shadow to sunbeam, bird-cry to distant traffic, day to night. And she was a small thing on the grass, alone in the careless sundown. And Harrison was coming, and with him would come the half-glance and the cautious word, the slip and the recovery, the tension that filled the house and brought the horror home.

Hugo was right. A week longer, and she would break, and all this would be over. Another note from Roy, another trial by tension like she had stood to-day at the restaurant, and she would snap and she would tell Harrison everything. She would scream it at him because she would be powerless, a child crying aloud and releasing all that tortured its frightened mind.

"You ought to go away," his voice floated down to her. She looked up, and the sun's light sparkled across the cut glass he held. "Somewhere just for a while, by yourself."

"*Othello* opens this week. I can't."

"After you've seen the first night. Go on Saturday morning." He sat down again in the deck-chair, leaning his forearms on his knees, letting the glass dangle from the fingers of one hand.

"Saturday morning? That's the last of the four days you've given yourself."

"Even so, you can take it as a coincidence. I'm not asking you to go away because on that last day I expect to find Roy. I don't; but you should still go. Stay here and things will happen. You can feel that."

"Yes, I can feel it. A creeping thing. It isn't nice. I get fancies. About Harrison and Roy and Helen Ledine and—Hugo, what do you know of Helen Ledine?"

"Little. I've met her once and she's come to my flat once."

"Did you ask her to?"

"No."

"What do you think of her?"

"Vital, histrionic, lives on the edge of her nerves—"

"Does she know where Roy is?"

The surface of her gin shivered. He said:

"Who is Roy?"

"I can't just forget him, not in a minute. Does she know where Roy is?"

"No."

"She could be hiding him—they used to be . . . together."

"He's not at her flat. I followed her there when she left mine."

"Did she see you?"

"No. She doesn't know where Roy is, Nicole. Try to forget him."

"It's asking too much," she said impatiently.

"You're trying too little." He decided suddenly that the time for gentleness was past. To reach the core of this emotional tumour he must use a blade. "If you don't forget him, I'll leave you no choice. I'm sorry."

"Aren't you taking too much on?"

"Yes, but I'm taking it off you. Forget Trafford. He isn't worth it."

"I pay the price."

"The goods are rotten. When you left his dressing-room on the last night you saw him, Helen went there to him."

All things ebbed from her voice but preparedness for shock. Like a ship that has stowed canvas and awaits the storm, she was calm, and patient.

"Did she tell you that?"

"I know it. They went to his hotel together on

173

that evening." He looked at his shoes. On his left shoe an ant was darting, tiny and black and fretful on the bright leather. "She stayed the night."

The ant reached the laces and reared, and some strange decision entered the minute intellect, for it turned and busily hastened away towards the toe.

Softly she whispered, "I don't believe that."

"You don't want to."

"You're just trying to set me against him, to make me forget him."

"Yes I am. But not with any lies. You'll both have to forget him, you and Helen. I believe he's dead."

Too swiftly—"No! His letters—he wanted to see me to-day—"

"The letters are from someone else."

"Who?"

"I shall soon know."

Silence came back, save for the faint jarring of a radio-station that was squeaking from the open kitchen-window. The sound crept round the house like a freak escaped. He turned his head.

The dying sun burned in her green eyes; they stared at him. They were wide, and clear, and horror was there. Her sweet mouth passed the words softly, speaking them as if she read them from a book whose meaning puzzled her.

"Has Helen murdered?"

"I shall know soon. I don't think it was Helen."

Blood had left her face. She did not move. She said:

"At last you've said something that I could believe is true. But . . . there are so many things—"

"There are always so many things that point away from murder when murder's done, because people always try to head us off."

"Hugo, now that you have told me what's in your mind, there's something I must—"

Her small head swung and the dark moving hair was sunshot as it left the edge of shadow from the cedar-tree. From the drive the sound came of wheels moving over loose gravel.

"Expect that's Harrison," he said.

She said, "Yes, I expect it is."

11th

MOVE

 LATER THEY BROUGHT a narrow table on
to the lawn, and drew chairs to it. The
sun was almost down but the air and the evening
were heavy with its heat; its heat lingered on faces,
beat against the temples and the eyeballs, swam in
the twilight on the mellow stones.

A wash of clear illumination was shed from the
glass doors of the loggia, and on the chequered
board the shadows of the pieces were elongated
and grotesque because of this slanting light. The
Pawns sat with narrow necks and behind them the
Bishops loomed, pious and prurient and watchful.
The Rooks were thin and graceful in their slender
shadow-form, the Knights were as long as shep-
herds' crooks. The King and Queen that stood near-

est the light's source were already slim, so that their shadows had lost their heads beyond the board's far boundary.

The two men smoked, Pedley a cigar, Bishop a pipe. They looked down at the battlefield, and at the serried armies there.

They had drawn colours; it was Pedley's gambit.

His hand's shadow fluttered over the board, and fled.

White had moved Pawn to Queen-four.

In the calm green of her watching eyes, Nicole's thoughts came, for no one was looking. She gazed at the chess board, the red pieces and the ivory, and remembered that she must say to Hugo what she had had to break off. There had been a little time, when Harrison had driven to the porch, to tell Hugo; but it would have left them no time in which to lift their minds from so much secrecy, to greet Harrison as they must, quite naturally.

But she must tell him about Helen, and what Helen had said that night. It would help him to find Roy, to find if he lived or was dead.

The evening lowered, and the shafts of lamplight grew brighter from the doors. On the board another Pawn had moved. She watched the profiles of the two faces, and the shadows on the squares, and the creeping of smoke from the cigar and the ghost-white pipe's bowl; and the squares grew blurred, white merging with black, red with ivory; and the smoke crept in sly grey skeins on the heavy air; and she remembered Helen.

Against the staccato beat of the swing-band she remembered Helen, in the stifling haze of cigarette-smoke, the scent of alcohol. Helen with the cool, clear voice.

"With Roy?"

The bubble-lights swung, their coloured balloons floating over the dancers and showing up a face inane with laughter, another set in a semi-drunken frown, a third as blank as the drum.

"Yes."

Helen nodded, as though she understood. She tilted the unlit cigarette. "Do you have a light, Mrs. Pedley?"

Her low voice had lingered over the title. It was the only real word in the sentence; and it seemed to echo.

Nicole passed the small gold lighter from her bag. "Thanks."

The music pulsed, was pumped out of the brass throats and the drum-lung; it had the cohesion and the discordancy of breaking glass. Helen passed back the lighter and said:

"He'll be back in a minute. Before he comes I

want to ask you something. D'you think you're in love with him?"

Nicole was in love with him, was confident, was on top of a world she had never known existed. She wasn't afraid of anyone in it.

"Isn't that rather my own affair?"

"Oh, quite. And not your first, I imagine. But you see I've been in love with Roy ever since I met him. That was three months ago. He feels like that about me, too."

The rhythm writhed. Light shone down on a dusky face with flashing eyes and gleaming teeth; he was a jungle-boy in well-cut cloth, singing like a Saturday night for a liquored crowd. The dancers wreathed, their feet slopping to the sugar-music.

"Roy has said nothing about you," Nicole said.

"No, he wouldn't have. But Mrs. Pedley, I'm saying this. I don't mind his playing around. I do it myself, it's fun. But nothing permanent, please. If you're thinking of keeping him, change your mind."

"I think we'll talk to him about it, shall we? He has a mind, too."

"I'm not staying. I never bust into his casual affairs. That's one of the reasons we stay in love. All I want to tell you is that if you're going to try to keep him, you're going to fail."

The lights veered, mazing among the swaying faces; the rhumba drummed red-hot from the reeds. Helen looked at Nicole with a calm face and steady eyes. "Mrs. Pedley, I'm keeping that boy for life. If I can't nobody else will have him. Not alive." She looked over the swaying heads, and turned away slowly. "Would you remember that?"

As Roy came between the scattered tables she smiled and moved her cigarette in a friendly wave. He smiled back, lifting a hand, as she went towards the alcove tables.

"Sorry I kept you waiting, my sweet. The operator was tangled up in their wires."

Nicole said, "That's all right." He led her to a vacant square-foot on the packed floor, and they began to dance. It was a shuffle, a mere movement of limbs to music. Only the coloured lights were free as they floated like magical bubbles. "Roy, I've just been talking to Helen."

"Yes, I saw."

"She said you still love her."

He smiled. "I expect she did." He was taller than she, so that his dark magnificent face was tilted down, and the long eyes like Aquila's were almost closed. A glint of gentle amusement between the lashes was all she saw. "But she says that to everyone, about everyone."

"She seemed utterly serious."

"Oh, she is. She really goes to town on any new part she plays. The present one is that of the rejected lover, but give her a couple of days and she'll work up a temperature for someone else, and slide smoothly into the skin of a blushing young first-time-ever."

They were pressed against a wall of bodies whose mass vibrated with a slow sensual periodicy. The trumpeter's eyes bulged at the crowd, bulbous and blood-veined, and he lifted his instrument and pointed its wide-mouthed nozzle at the highest of the coloured lights, and played the final note of the number. It rang, this final note, like the scream of an animal. The scream was squeezed through the brass and was torn from it into the sticky air. It had a hideous frenzy in its one single long-drawn lifted howl, and when it stopped it was like a bullet collapsing a lung as the bang of the drum broke the scream of the brass and silence came.

Those who could raise their hands clapped with a bored automatic indifference. Nicole said:

"I wonder if you really know Helen."

"I know them all."

She frowned, trying to keep the confidences that seemed so unassailable.

"Darling, I know you're the Great Lover, but let's not think it's everything."

"What? Oh, no—I mean I know all the Helens." The music began again, grunting into the murmur with an urgent bestial beat. "You said you wondered if I knew Helen. There are so many Helens, and I know them all. Don't worry, she's really quite sweet and enjoys talking to people as long as they'll listen. Just now she's the spurned lover. Next week she'll have forgotten my name."

Nicole danced mechanically; some of her confidence in him was lost; but Helen Ledine and her words fitted into this pattern so well—the swinging lamps, the beating rhythm, the liquor and the laughter—that outside its hysterical context the warning she had given would seem absurd. Tomorrow it would seem absurd.

"Roy, shall we go?

"If you like. Where to?"

"Anywhere away from this."

"Sorry, I thought you might enjoy it."

"I have."

They left. They didn't see Helen as they went out. Perhaps she had gone too.

Pedley murmured "Check." His voice came through a cloud to Nicole, and she saw the board again. Time had passed; she had not known.

Bishop took a white Pawn *en passant* and covered his King. In the deck-chair, Nicole shivered. The heat of the day had gone, and the air was cool. She left the lawn, and came down later with a wrap. The two men had stopped playing. The game had lasted an hour and a half.

"Good one?" she said, lighting a cigarette.

"Splendid, my dear. Mr. Bishop has the cunning of an adept. His surprises are superb."

"In fact," Bishop said cheerfully, "I nearly won the game..."

A rich rumble of humour came from Pedley.

"Little matter who wins, it's the battle that warms the heart. Now we must celebrate a good campaign."

Nicole was warm again, and wondered why she had gone in for the wrap. The air felt close, still; it had been her thoughts that had brought the unnatural chill. She chose to drink a rum, and listened for a while to Pedley talking of *Othello*, and of the play he was writing himself—

"In three Acts, conventionally enough; but so far I cannot see the third very clearly."

"That's traditional, isn't it?" said Bishop.

"It is. Indeed, I have almost reached the curtain of Act Two; and where I shall go from there I'm not sure. It may never come to me. In which case the play will never be seen by anyone." His voice brooded, and he spoke almost to himself. "Never be seen, never heard of, never remembered..."

"What does your critic say about it so far?"

"My critic?" He understood, and smiled. "Even my critic has not seen a word of it."

"Which means," Nicole said, "that it's probably shaping well. It's when Harrison gets into a mess that he calls me in."

"Such is your unenviable lot, dear Nicole. Even so, there's another reason for my reticence. I am writing the tragedy in ordinary prose at the moment, as one would write a diary. Then I shall see it as a whole if it is ever finished, and so select my scenes and montages. For the present I must content myself with Shakespeare for actual production. I could do worse."

He had dismissed his own writing too casually; and there seemed to be a place for further interest. Bishop said:

"Is yours a period play?"

"The time is to-day. The characters are ordinary people. I know them well. Their problems are expounded in the first two Acts, and the resolution is to be made in the last. Time will show me the best way for them, perhaps; if not, I shall drop the script into the furnace and submit their problems to the devil."

"It would be galling if he found the answer," said Bishop, "where it had eluded you."

"If he did, Mr. Bishop, I should offer him my soul for the third Act." His low chuckle rumbled again in the quiet air. "Plus a ten per cent cut of gross receipts."

"An unusual offer."

"For an unusual play. One day I must show you the script, if it is ever completed. I'd welcome your good opinion."

Bishop left before eleven. There had been no chance of talking alone to Nicole, even for a moment. Whatever she had been going to say, when Pedley's arrival had interrupted her, must wait. The grey saloon whispered through the gates like a wraith in the moonlight; the ruby tail-lamp winked and vanished, and the drive was quiet again save for their footsteps as Harrison and his wife crossed the cold stones of the porch, and closed the door.

"Tired, my dear?"

The hall was dimly lighted, and the panelling held the day's warmth.

"A little."

He touched her arm affectionately.

"I'll be up later. My brain is still busy. I shan't disturb you."

"You never do. Don't make it too late, Harrison. Long day to-morrow."

"I know."

She went up the stairs, turning once and giving him the last smile that was due to him to-day; then she reached the landing, hating herself because it had been so hard to give. On Saturday she'd go away for a little, after the first night was over. Hugo was right; she must get away soon, and try to leave Roy behind her when she came back, or he'd be with her always here in this house, and Harrison would know.

Below her room, as she undressed and creamed

her makeup off, Pedley turned on the small lamp over his writing-desk and unlocked the middle drawer. He placed the heavy book gently on to the desk and opened it at the marker. Then, with his fountain-pen, he began writing. His face was expressionless as the shadow of his hand moved with a slow and steady rhythm across the page.

Bishop had stayed in his flat all the morning because he knew she would phone him there. It was at eleven o'clock. They asked each other how they were and then she said:

"Hugo, it doesn't seem so important now, but you ought to hear it. It's about Helen Ledine. Soon after Roy and I sort of became in love, she told me I was poaching on her preserves."

She gave a brittle laugh, as if in apology. The words she had just uttered were cheap words, out of a smart novelette. She had tried to make it all sound light and off-hand, but that was how it sounded. She felt like a country-girl telling her uncle that it was the farmer's boy who'd got her into trouble.

Understandingly Bishop said, "I see, yes. It doesn't surprise me."

"She said if he left her, she'd kill him."

Did the drama of that lessen the cheapness? Little.

"Did she really say that?"

There was a long pause. Then her voice was not humiliated nor apologetic.

"Hugo, if you don't believe things I say, there's no one else I can talk to. And it helps so much."

"You mustn't be so quick, and I mustn't phrase things so ambiguously. I meant did Helen actually say she'd kill him—in so many words? Or did she just throw a violent act and become melodramatic?"

"She was quite calm. Roy dismissed it—"

"You told him what she'd said?"

She thought carefully, trying to remember.

"No. I think I told him that Helen seemed to be still in love with him."

"Ah. And he shrugged it off."

"Yes."

"Have you seen Helen since then? To talk to?"

"No."

"Has she ever written to you or given you any indication that she was serious about killing him?"

"No."

"Do you think she has?"

The silence began to lengthen. The telephone in his hand became like an emptying tunnel, black and plastic and shadowed. He visualized her small slim figure, running down the tunnel away from his question, looking over her shoulder with a white little frightened face in case he asked her again. When her voice filled the tunnel again it was like a fleeting echo.

"I don't know. I don't think I care."

He answered her softly, and gently, because he heard the hopeless tremor in her voice. She was a long way from him, in a phone-box, very alone and bewildered. In another moment she might let the receiver fall and press her shoulder against the heavy door, and walk over the pavement, and cross the road without looking, without knowing, without caring. When the tyres shrilled the receiver would be swinging on its flex, slower and slower. Then it would stop, and the long thin tunnel would really be empty.

"Nicole, it doesn't really matter where Roy is, and it doesn't matter about Helen. You've gone into a cinema just because there was nothing else to do. The film's a wash-out; it isn't worth the price of the seat. You ought to leave now. You won't go back because it'll mean getting another ticket, and the thing won't be any better. Just chuck it, Nicole."

She was over-controlling her voice. The words came in little gusts and were clipped off with a desperate precision.

"I—can't. I can't chuck it, he's written to me again."

"A letter this morning?"

"Yes."

"Can you tell me what it says?"

"He was there yesterday."

"At the Honey Pot?"

"Yes. He saw me sitting there with Harrison. He nearly came up to our table because he was so furious."

"Don't leave anything out." He listened so intently that when Vera Gorringe knocked and came into the room he did not know. Nicole was telling him that Trafford was murdered, and she was telling him the name of his murderer as clearly as though her voice had pronounced its syllables. "You needn't quote from the letter," he said, "but don't leave anything out."

"Well he just left. He picked up my note."

"Which note?"

Miss Gorringe went out and closed the door. He looked up, and when he realised that she had come and gone he pressed a bell-push in the knee-hole of the desk.

"Didn't I tell you?" In her voice he could see her hand pass over her brow. She was beginning not to remember small important things. She was beginning not to care. "When Harrison went to our table I left him, and scribbled a note to Roy, in the cloakroom. I left it at the desk before I joined Harrison again."

Miss Gorringe came in, looked across the long room, then closed the door and sat on the davenport, and picked up *The Listener*. *The Times* would be too large and noisy. She heard the undertone of excitement in his voice, and knew that nothing must interrupt.

"What does his letter say, about the note?"

"Just that he collected it."

"Did he know it was there for him?"

"He probably thought I'd managed to leave one, to explain why Harrison was with me. Does it matter?"

"No, nothing matters. Is that everything in the letter?"

She spoke like an automaton, or as though she were being questioned under the influence of a truth-drug.

"No. He asked me for money. For fifty pounds."

"Was it to be sent to Tallow Lane, as before?"

"Yes."

"Does he suggest a new appointment, to meet you?"

"No. He says he won't risk it again."

He thought for a while before he spoke again, and she could not wait for him. "Hugo, please tell me what I shall do."

"That won't be easy for you. I want you to turn the whole thing over to me entirely, and forget it as much as you can."

"You keep saying that."

"I know. And you keep not doing it. Now I can persuade you. I've had information this morning.

I'm afraid Roy is dead. I can give you that quite cold, because you already knew it was a possibility."

He waited before going on. He had to have her reaction. Nothing came. He said: "Would you like to ring off and have a drink somewhere? I could meet you in a few minutes if you're in the West End."

After a bit she said in a thin voice:

"No. I'm all right. Go on."

"That's all. Roy won't ever meet you. He can't. These letters and appointment were someone else's doing. Forget Roy, forget the letters, forget everything except the first night on Friday. And go away on Saturday, as I've already suggested. Now can you try to do all that?"

"Yes, I can try."

She had answered more quickly. She sounded less bewildered, less hopeless. Something had been made definite. Roy was dead. She said again quietly, "Yes, I can try."

"Good. It'll be easier than it seems now. I'm sorry I had to tell you just when you were feeling so low, but it's better that you should know for certain. It's worse to go on hoping and wondering."

A little too brightly she said:

"Yes."

"Have you left the Parthenon, just now I mean?"

"Yes. Harrison is working. I'm in a box near by."

"Are you going back to watch rehearsals now?"

"I think so." With a quaint appeal in her voice that unsteadied him she asked, "I ought to, oughtn't I?"

"Yes. And leave everything in the phone-box. Let the door slam on it, bang."

Breathlessly she said, "All right."

After a moment the line clicked and went dead. When he cradled the receiver it was like interrupting someone who had been telling him a ghost story; but he was sure he knew the end. He looked up.

"Gorry, that was Nicole. I expect you heard. She's just told me who murdered Trafford."

Vera Gorringe closed *The Listener* and laid it on the davenport beside her. She said:

"So it's really murder."

"It is."

"Did she know she was telling you?"

"No."

"And she told you also who killed the boy?"

"Yes. But—" his hand moved to the telephone as it began ringing. With his hand on the dumb-bell he sat quite still for a moment and then said: "Take it for me, would you?"

She came across to the desk.

"In to nobody?" she asked.

"To nobody."

She picked up and said, "Miss Gorringe."

Bishop admired her blue-rinse in the sunshine, and wondered what Nicole would do when he had to tell her everything.

"I'm sorry, Inspector, he's out...I've no idea...Very well, I will. Good-bye."

Perhaps Nicole would be relieved, if her conscience let her be. It was a way out, and she'd have no choice but to take it.

He said, "Freddie?"

"Yes. He asked would you phone him when you got in."

"Thank you. I shan't do that."

She perched on the arm of a chair.

"Are you going to let him come in, now that you know everything?"

"No. Because I don't know everything. I only think I know. I can't tell Freddie yet. I can't tell you, either, because it's so fantastic that you'll start pointing out the anomalies. That would undermine the confidence I have in my being right."

"It might save you a lot of trouble."

"Not a lot, no. I shall know for certain by to-morrow night." He gazed at the jade figure on his desk. It was a little Chinese water-carrier, still, and green, and inscrutable. The water would never spill. "Are you going out this evening, Gorry?"

"Unless you want me here."

"No, but I shall be out too, so we must see to little Chu."

"I'll make sure she's not shut in."

Absently he murmured, "We should do that," and then his voice changed and became quick. "Gorry, you know most of this but I'd like you to see the whole picture of the scene and then tell me what you think of it. Yesterday morning Nicole had a letter from Trafford—which name will suffice for the sender—arranging to meet her at one o'clock the same day, at the Honey Pot in Gerrard Street. This was the result of her having asked him to arrange such a meeting. For some reason—possibly due to her reluctance to make Pedley suspicious—she went there, *with* Pedley, and I joined them fifteen minutes later.

"I had watched for a long time, sitting in the car within sight of the restaurant doorway. I did not see Trafford. When I sat down at the Pedleys' table I made sure of watching everyone who came in: I had my back to the middle of the room, but faced a wall mirror, which I was able to view without turning my head at all. I saw nothing of Trafford. Nor did Nicole—and she must have been watching too, far more anxiously than I. The three of us left together. Trafford had not come.

"By 'Trafford' I mean the sender of the letters, of course. But Nicole says that before sitting down with Pedley, she went into the cloakroom, wrote a note to Trafford explaining her husband's presence, and left it at the desk. She hoped that if Trafford came, and saw Pedley, he would leave right away, and think of asking if she had left a message for him.

"Trafford did come to the Honey Pot, and asked if there were a note, and collected it, and told Nicole in a letter she received this morning that he had done this."

He sat back tipping his fingers together. "Under my damned nose," he said quietly.

After silence had extended to a full minute, Miss Gorringe said:

"Is that all of the scene, Hugo?"

"It is."

"Trafford couldn't have seen Pedley or Nicole or you without your seeing him in the mirror? Without Nicole's seeing him?"

"That is right. He couldn't have."

She left the arm of the chair and began walking. The coin-bracelet she wore glittered in the sun's light as the pieces moved. "Suppose the note were picked up some time *after* you three had left?"

"It might have been—but unless Trafford had seen Pedley with her, why should he ask if there were a note for him?"

"Trafford might be someone who knew that they'd be there together."

"Someone, you mean, at the Parthenon—one of the cast, one of the technicians—"

"Any one of fifty people working on *Othello*."

He nodded. "That is possible, but I prefer another theory. That Trafford was in the restaurant all of the time. He might have gone in while I was watching from the car: I've no idea what he looks like."

She turned; the tiny bright coins were still.

"But you think you know who he is. Who killed the real Roy Trafford."

"Yes, I think I do. But I'm putting this to you as if I didn't. In a minute you're going to put your very practised finger on a salient spot: and if it points to Trafford's impostor—the person I'm thinking of— I shall buy you a bottle of *Paquin*. But you still won't know the actual name, and I shall, and that will give me a sense of childish triumph." His face was dead serious."

"You really mean, Hugo, that your theory is so absurd that I'll be contemptuous when you tell me."

"Yes, and I can stand anything but that. Have another go—you get five shies for sixpence."

"Very well. This person might have gone into the place while you were watching it. Or might have been there before you turned up. Or was certainly sitting there while you three were lunching."

"Good."

"And certainly, therefore, saw Pedley, and saw Nicole leaving something at the desk."

"Excellent."

"But all I'm doing is playing it your way, at your suggestion."

"If you saw the slightest false step in my reasoning, you'd have pulled me up by now."

"You can stop looking smug. The person we want has been cornered, because I think you're right in your general reasoning. But he's cornered either in the Parthenon or in the Honey Pot—possibly in both. He could be one of the theatre people, someone who went to the Honey Pot. That leaves you something like a hundred souls to search among."

She was a little disgruntled. Bishop seldom kept his aces hidden like this.

"A hundred," he said, "is a nice round figure. There are eight million in London. So we've narrowed down the area of search to one eighty-thousandth of the original. That's quite a fair morning's work."

She stopped pacing, and stood in front of the desk.

"All right, Hugo, I'm giving in. I think you've got something. I wish you'd tell me more, but I'll wait. Meanwhile, you've a murder on your hands. And a murderer."

He leaned back in the carved chair and held the tips of his fingers together. Over their raised steeple he looked up at her gravely.

"Yes. But don't tell me I must take care."

"I'm telling you exactly that. I've seen this happen before. I've seen you risk your neck in odd places. Will you at least carry a gun?"

His brow furrowed gradually, and an expression of severe pain bespread his lean face. He enunciated with extreme care.

"A—*gun*, Miss Gorringe?"

She gave a matter-of-fact nod.

"A gun," she said simply.

"And shall I wear a hat?" he asked gently, as if addressing a backward child, "a soft hat of very light grey colour, with a very wide brim cocked wickedly across the brow? Yes? And a tie, Miss Gorringe? One of those ties three feet long with hand-painted panoramas of beach-pyjama-clad Coney Island beauty-tootsies demonstrating the visual advantages of Uplift? Well, Miss Gorringe?"

"Have it your way," said Miss Gorringe.

He raised an eyebrow. "It certainly might be diverting, I admit. I can just *see* myself, walking down St. James's." He extended his hands, as a film director would frame a new scene as he developed its perspective—"down St. James's, my dear Vera ... with coffee-coloured play-shoes and chequerboard hose ... gaberdine pants and fancy neckwear ... shoulder-pads and sideboards ... and the hat—the *hat*, Vera dear—a hat to end all headgear, with a snap brim and pheasant's feather, a high crown and an art-silk band, a hat with such roguish poise, such wicked angle, such subtly suggestive tilt, a hat that is blocked, cocked and decked with such a saucy daring that no passer-by could fail to recognise its wearer: a million-buck private eye, a city-slicker gunning for a down-town sucker—Bishop, the Boy that Beats the Band!"

Miss Gorringe, who was now on the davenport, lowered *The Listener*, winced delicately, and returned her gaze to its pages.

"I only said you ought to be careful," she murmured.

Bishop lowered his arm from its lofty gesturing, took his foot off the desk, and sat down with a sigh.

"I will be careful, Mother dear."

He then relaxed, allowing himself a moment in which to complete the more serious picture that Nicole, without knowing, had given him. If his theory were right, he knew many things that recently had been a mystery. He knew all about the courteous little seedsman in Tallow Lane; he knew why the appointment to meet Nicole had been made in yesterday's letter . . . and why it had seemingly not been kept; he knew where Roy Trafford's body lay on this sunny London morning. This last was known only to one other person in the world; and that person's name was known—as a murderer's—only to Bishop.

He moved in the chair, inwardly fascinated by the fantastic conception that had been revealed to him: a conception achieved in high passion, whose child was murder, a child sired by jealousy and born in fiendish hate.

Then he stopped thinking, and relaxed. He could do little for a while. Meantime, his pipe had gone out. He touched the cooling tobacco with a match's flame, and looked across at Vera Gorringe. She was reading, and—he knew quite well—sulking, because he had refused to tell her everything, and because he had scorned her idea of carrying a gun.

As he looked at her his expression changed.

The grey eyes narrowed and the lean jaw set in a grim line. He took his *meerschaum* and held it by the bowl, turning it upside-down. Slowly, with deadly deliberation, he pointed the stem at the unsuspecting woman on the davenport, and then took meticulous aim through the wisp of smoke that curled up from the mouthpiece. Posed as rigidly as the figure of doom, he drew a sharp, audible breath.

Miss Gorringe looked up.

"Bang!" he said loudly.

Miss Gorringe leapt.

12th

MOVE

BISHOP WORE NO TILTED HAT as he left his flat to meet the murderer, nor was there a gun in his pocket. He thought it possible— no more—that there would be danger to-night; but thought also that there were some occasions when the brain served better than a bullet.

Heat was spread like a bright hood over London; you could not glimpse the sky because of its own appalling glare. Dust did not stir along the gutters; in the squares and gardens dogs lay prone, tongues lolling, eyes bemused. Only cats did not seem aware of the oppressive heat, but then cats are seldom aware of anything save their secret moods.

Bishop took his car, because his route to the door of the murderer was devious. In the back of the grey Rolls-Royce was an oblong box.

He turned into Charing Cross Road and parked for a moment by the island's triangle; for this moment he sat thinking, covering the ground ahead before he trod it, because in places there might be pits dug where the grass appeared most firm. Then the saloon murmured away, swinging left and nosing into the narrow channels of the side-streets.

Later it pulled up, and Bishop got out. He left the oblong box on the rear seat, and locked the doors because its contents were precious. Then he went into the stage door, and talked to the man there, finally going into the long stone corridor and walking steadily until he came to the small white label with the two names.

He knocked. A voice called out, asking him to go in.

They were both dressed. He closed the door after him and said:

"Good evening."

Miss Townend perked her bustle archly. "Lovely surprise!" she said. Then she went on with her corsage.

Helen Ledine was looking into the mirror at Bishop. As Lady Diana she was wearing an enormous hat, ponderous with feathers. It changed her appearance incredibly, after his last sight of her in the flat. She said:

"We're on in fifteen minutes."

He hesitated, wondering whether it mattered that the other woman was here; then he decided that it did not. His voice was quiet, and a little cold.

"I've just discovered who killed Trafford, Helen."

Miss Townend gave an audible squeak, Helen Ledine did not turn, but stared at him in the mirror, her eyes almost expressionless; almost, save for the hint of fright. Then it faded and the face became mask-like with its heavy make-up and the great feathered hat.

"What do you want me to do—fall on my hat-pin?"

As if she had remained silent he added:

"So that I shall now have to hand the whole thing over to the Yard. I thought you should know."

Audrey Townend gaped over her billowing corsage; but her bewilderment was genuine. "For God's sake," she said with a gooseberry mouth, "What—"

"Now that you've passed the time of day," Helen's brittle tone cut in, "you'd better go and finish your Edgar Wallace in the woodshed. Nanny won't ever look for you there. I said we're on in fifteen minutes."

The imperceptible nervous trembling of her body was made perceptible by the absurd hat and its high feathers; their sensitive tips exaggerated the trembling like a seismograph. He was satisfied.

"Then I won't disturb you any longer," he said

gently, and turned to the door. Her voice ricochetted from the bright hard mirror.

"What makes you imagine I'm disturbed?"

He opened the door. He said, "I was thinking of Miss Townsend, too. She is also on in fifteen minutes, I assume."

"Townend," Miss Townend said in a high-pitched, puzzled tone.

"Townend, I beg your pardon."

He closed the door, and walked back along the passage. In his tiny office, the door-keeper sat reading a paper. He looked up, shaking his grey head.

"Still don't see it, sir. Say what you like."

Bishop stopped, leaning on the door-jamb so that he was not in sight of the passage.

"Well, we shall see on Saturday," he said easily. "If they keep Blackwell in the forward line it'll be a walk-over."

The man sucked his teeth.

"Las' game of the season an' all?" he said. "Never on your life. Too much at stake, see?"

Bishop formed a reply, then dismissed it, unspoken. In the confines of the near-distance he had heard the opening of the door; and now the footsteps, the quick, clipped footsteps that neared rapidly.

"An' again," the old man said, "if they're goin' to risk leavin' Blackwell in the forwards, 'stead of using him where he can do more damage, they'll—"

The footsteps stopped and Helen's expression set in the instant as she saw Bishop. The long feathers bobbed for a moment longer and then were placid.

Bishop straightened up from the door-jamb and gestured politely towards the little office. Looking at her pale, over-painted face he addressed the door-keeper quietly.

"Miss Ledine would like to telephone. Good night."

He went out, crossing the narrow dusty pavement and passing the grey saloon, walking on towards the corner, where the phone-box stood. Inside, he dialled the number of the Parthenon Theatre. After a moment a man's voice said:

"Mr. Pedley, sir? He went off—o—o—half-hour ago."

"Was he going home, d'you know?"

"Think so, sir. I thought I heard him say that."

"Thank you."

Bishop depressed the contact, waited, put in four more pennies, and dialled the Hampstead number. In a few seconds the engaged-tone was humming in his ear. He cradled the instrument and left the box after Button-B-ing his coppers back. He would want them again. At this moment, four simple pennies were most important.

For five minutes he strolled in the side-street, thinking over the fact that Helen seemed to have known that Harrison Pedley would not be at the

Parthenon just now; she had obviously got straight on to the house. But that could only have been a good guess, or the selection of the probable, because to-morrow night was the first night of the new *Othello*, and nobody could say at any give time where Pedley would be. It would depend upon how rehearsals were going at the eleventh hour.

He did not worry about her telephoning Hampstead. He would have worried had she not done that. He had expected that she would, and she was, so that was all right. Another point had been confirmed, another small unit of the jig-saw was fitting snugly into its place; and the final assembly was already clear. The face in the hypo was no longer an indistinct image.

Bishop went back in five minutes, and from the house in Hampstead the maid spoke. He asked for her mistress. In a little while he heard Nicole's soft voice.

"This," he said gently, "is Hugo. How are you?"

"Better." But still shaky, still with the ground sliding away from her feet. He heard it in the one soft word of reply.

"Good. Forgive me if I don't talk long—would you mind meeting me at the Dutch Inn this evening?"

"When?"

"As soon as you can manage."

After a pause: "I—could come right away, if you want."

"That would be nice. I'll go there now, and wait."

As though she suddenly regretted her hasty compliance she said, "You must see me—alone? Or would you like to come up here?"

"I think the Inn might be better."

"All right, I'll come."

"Fine. In about twenty minutes?"

"Yes, in twenty minutes."

He rang off. She had wanted to ask more, to ask why, but that could wait until they met. It wasn't very important; after what Hugo had told her earlier to-day, little else was important. Roy was dead.

Bishop went to the car and sat there for some ten minutes, then went back to the telephone. When the maid answered again he asked for Mr. Pedley. Harrison came on.

"Bishop here, sir."

"Ah, Mr. Bishop. How are you—we saw nothing of you at the theatre to-day?"

"I had to forgo that pleasure. Rehearsals are going well?"

"Splendidly."

"I'm glad. I wondered if I might show you the result of my bidding yesterday. Unless of course you're resting after the day's work."

"Bidding, Mr. Bishop?"

"At Waring's; the ivory pieces—"

"Of course, the pieces! I should be quite delighted to see them, and of course to see you."

"Thank you. At what time?"

"At once, if that suits you."

"It does. In a few minutes, then."

"In a few minutes, my dear Bishop; I shall be most excited."

When Bishop started his engine he thought of Nicole again, and the lean saloon swung from the narrow lanes to the wider thoroughfares towards the Dutch Inn. With the doorman he left a brief note before returning to the car and driving for Hampstead. He was not pleased with himself, but it had been necessary to avoid a risk. Had he asked her simply to leave the house, she would have been too puzzled. Asking her to meet him was more casual, less demanding; she would have to forgive the deception that the brief note would expose.

He was glad that she had not told her husband where she was going; upon that much he had relied, and not in vain. Pedley would have been surprised by his telephone call had he heard from Nicole that she was going out to meet him at the Dutch Inn.

Hampstead was cooler, greener, loftier than the lower streets and buildings. The sun, already dipping to its riotous climax among the horizon's clouds, was now oblique and merciful; but the air was not clear. Night was coming like a sly headache, still burdened by the day's heat.

The reflection of the ivy that massed the house

washed over the grey cellulose, as wind ruffles a grey sea. The engine died, and silence throbbed in its place. Bishop did not hear the door of the house open; when he got out of the car he saw Harrison Pedley, standing on the porch.

He was in a white linen suit, a plump, flabby figure with a half-smile and an outstretched hand.

"You have not been long, Mr. Bishop."

"It isn't far."

He took the fleshy hand, and felt moisture on his own as he withdrew it. "I wondered that you felt like viewing a few pieces of ivory, at such short notice. You must be on edge about to-morrow's first night."

"I relax occasionally, and what better relaxation than in the company of a quiet voice and the sight of antique artistry?" He laid a hand on Bishop's shoulder. "Come in, come in, and we shall borrow just one fleeting hour's dream from the clock's amassing hoard." His chuckle was plump like his hand as he guided his guest through the dark-panelled hall. "Or more simply, grab time by its accursed forelock and yank it away for a while..."

The room was cooler than the drive, for the sun had slid too far round to glare longer through the windowpanes. Pedley offered a drink, but Bishop declined as he laid the oblong box on the writing-desk.

"The condition," he murmured, "is less fine than

that of the set we played with here last night; but something can be done in the way of cleaning up." He raised the lid.

For a while Pedley said nothing, but watched his guest take each piece from the box and lay it on the leather covering of the desk-top. The ivory was discoloured, and one carved banner of a Rook was broken; but the set was magnificent. The Pawns were infantrymen with spears; the Knights were cavalry; the Bishops, Queens and Kings superb figures in sculpted robes and with delicately chiselled features. The Rooks were carried upon the backs of majestic elephants, and from the turret of each was raised a banner, its folds stiffened outwards to a wind.

"Exquisite."

It was the first word that either man had spoken for minutes. It came softly from Pedley. "I do congratulate you, my dear Bishop. You have a set to be proud of." A smile puckered his plump mouth. "And of course you had to pay for it..."

"Not outrageously. Twenty pounds."

The heavy eyebrows raised, the round head tilted.

"Very reasonable. I envy you not only the purchase but the price. You had a good day."

He fingered the pieces, turning them; and the love of their detail was clearly genuine; the deep brown eyes were soft as the large hands held the carvings tenderly.

"I had a good day," nodded Bishop, and began to fill his pipe. He was pleased that Pedley admired the pieces; their small quiet presence in this room might lessen the other: the presence of the ghost whose name would be voiced in a moment now. "And now I'm to have a bad evening, which is a pity." He sat, without invitation, in an easy-chair, and crossed his legs, and lit the tobacco in his pipe.

Pedley moved from the desk, still holding a red Knight, still admiring its detail, its proportions. Slowly he lowered his bulk to a chair opposite Bishop's and did not look at Bishop, but still at the piece in his hand. His murmur was idle.

"Oh, not essentially a bad evening, Mr. Bishop . . . not bad in every respect, m'm?" His chuckle broke again. "But then nothing is ever totally bad; one can always find balm where there is a barb . . ."

He studied with his narrowed brown eyes the sculpted figure of the horseman in his hand, and his hand, upon a sudden whim, turned it until the tiny arrow in the horseman's bow was pointed directly between his brooding eyes.

"How long," Bishop said, "have you been expecting me?"

Pedley placed the red Knight upon the arm of his chair, and for a moment allowed his gaze to linger on its crimson carving; then the round head swung, and the eyes looked to Bishop's; and in the room there came a tension almost tangible.

Neither had moved, but they had changed irrevocably. They were no longer two men sitting, the host and his guest. They were like two duellists who had chosen their weapons, who had taken their correct paces, who had now turned, and were facing.

The words fell gently in the quiet room.

"How long have I been expecting you, Mr. Bishop?" The fat hand moved in a slight shrug on the padded arm of the chair. "Not long. Not very long. Perhaps an hour. An hour ago I did not expect you at all."

Bishop's eyes did not leave the other's face.

"And now?" he said.

"And now, my dear Bishop, I stand in mortal danger." A queer smile in which no mirth moved was suddenly on the fleshy mouth, and as suddenly gone. "And so do you."

13th
MOVE

IN THE CARVED HAND of the tiny archer, the bow was bent and the string taut and the arrow fixed and aimed. But the shaft would never fly. Just as the little jade water-carrier upon Bishop's desk would never spill his burden, the red Knight's arrow would never dart.

Harrison Pedley looked at it.

"You came here to talk," he murmured. "I am listening."

The arches of his heavy brows were lifted as the deep brown eyes observed the Knight. In the eyes was danger, but not for the Knight.

"I came here simply to ask you something."

"I shall not answer you."

"You must—"

213

"On whose compulsion?"

"On your own."

The duellists paused, retiring, eyeing each other warily. Bishop was cautious, controlled; Pedley's rich tones possessed a dull indifference, a brutish arrogance, a refusal to recognise his situation.

Thrust again: "Where is Trafford?"

The big head swung. "Trafford?" Something of a smile was altering the shape of the slack fleshy mouth again, and the same mouth played with the name like a broken toy. "Trafford...oh, that boy..."

Bishop felt a strange chill moving down his nape. In the immobility, in the calm, in the casual attitude of the man there lay a hint of something hideous, a mind made mad. Yet Pedley was sane.

"Trafford," Bishop said slowly, "is more important than that."

"To me?" The smile laughed. "That boy?"

"To you, that boy. He's your master. There's no escaping him now. You know that."

"Strange fancies wreath your mood; your talk is fabulous."

"It is; I talk of a fabulous thing. Death, and despair, and a shattered heart. Stop your dreaming, Pedley, and wake. Look at the daylight."

"Damn your soul."

"What happens to my soul won't affect you. Wake up, and look at what's happened. You haven't long to live."

"I live how long I like!" The rich tones pitched and fury came into them like frenzied reeds along a bitter wind. "While there's poetry to shape, I live! I have my work, my life!"

"Your life is nearing an end, and so is your work. Wake up now and watch the world go out while you've a moment left."

The fat man shivered, and for minutes was silent. The round brown eyes brooded against Bishop's across the little distance that was all their barrier. The slack mouth was puckered like a sulky child's. The breathing was fast; the nostrils trembled; the plump pale hands fluttered on the arms of the chair and then at last—"*The Lord God damn your soul!*"

Bishop waited patiently. From the day-long dream of jealousy, and revenge, and ghoulish pleasuring, the mind of the man had passed to a nightmare unimagined; and for a little moment there would be a rioting of senses, a vortex of panic. While it span itself to exhaustion it was impossible to approach with words.

On the shelf above the hearth a clock ticked. In the grounds a bird cried. On the arm of the chair the tiny archer flexed his silent bow, his threat absurd in the presence of the huge maelstrom of Pedley's mind.

A minute passed. Sweat beaded the pale brow; the eyes' lids lowered and became hoods; and at last the hands were still, and bright with a clammy sheen.

In the other chair the padding rustled as Bishop moved, taking his match-box and striking a match, holding its flame over the white bowl of the pipe.

"Now we can talk more reasonably," he murmured.

"There's nothing to be said."

"Trafford's dead. You killed him."

"I shall not answer."

"There was no question. I stated it. You killed the boy. Where is he now?"

"In hell's nursery for brats."

"His body, then?"

"His body..." the brown eyes brooded, and the voice spoke half in reverie. "His body it was that wrought the evil...it was the animal she loved. His body was young, and blinded her to his mind—the mind of a simple idiot! The boy was a puling troubadour, and she went to him from me!"

Bishop slid the match-box to his pocket.

"Poetry isn't all, Pedley. Animals have blood in them. Your Bard knows that."

"I loved her with all my mind."

"That was the trouble. She's too young to learn a love like that, too young even to want it, yet. The tragedy started when you met, not now."

The acknowledgment was uttered on a sigh.

"It was then, I know. I know that now."

"Tell me, where is Trafford?"

"That is the least of matters." The heavy head

moved, tilting a little; the eyes held puzzlement. "Who are you?"

"A man, sorry for others."

"Save your pity."

"Without pity, life would be an engine run amok. Nobody would care, even for themselves. You have to have a brake, and pity's that."

"For your age, young man, you've more sense in you than Trafford had."

"Oh, I'm not an oracle—"

"You haven't told me who you are."

"My name and what I am, how I was born, what I live for—those are trivialities to you. They don't mean anything. There's no point in telling you."

"But what have you done—that means everything, even to me, a stranger."

"I've planned your death, I give you that. I'm sorry, but someone else would have done that, if I hadn't. You planned Trafford's, I've planned yours. You're a poet, and there's poetic justice for you."

"There's no rhyme in it—"

"There's reason, there's the law."

"A fool thing, designed for automata whose pattern's the same. It wasn't made for people. That fool of a boy broke something magical, it's right that he should die—"

"No, it's wrong, by law and by simple justice. The magic was all yours, it wasn't shared. You thought she loved you as you loved her, on a plane quite

different from an animal's. You asked too much of
a girl—"

"I gave—"

"You gave the things she never wanted alone.
With the other things she craved, the magic could
have mixed; but you were a blind apothecary. No
fault of yours, you needn't blame yourself."

"There's no question of blame for anyone.
Whoever made the world made a medley, and I am
one of those who are out of tune."

With a suddenness that startled Bishop the rich
tones broke and the bland white face was buried
in the fat white hands, and for a moment the slack
body could not be still though it made no sound.
This was a horror that Pedley had never envisaged,
and it was thrusting through him like a cleaving
blade. The horror of being lost, and alone at last.

The clock ticked on the mantelpiece; the bird was
gone from the garden; and then the horror passed.
The hands tumbled from the face and the face
looked into Bishop's, and the voice was strong
again.

"Who else knows what I did?"

"No one."

"No one else?"

"I am the only one."

In the brief silence the thought crept, undis-
guised, like a beggar whose rags were a trade-
mark, not a shame.

"Only you . . ."

Bishop was not tensed; there would be time. Pedley had no weapon that was visible. His mind, clearing of the horror that had swamped it through, was now alert again, and reasoning. The thought that had come to it had been there once before, when Trafford had been done to death by these plump white hands. It was thought of murder.

"But what's the point?" asked Bishop evenly.

"The point?" The eyes were bright.

"Of killing me. It wouldn't work. You've done it once, and everything's been lost. By doing the same thing again you can't get the other back."

"She would love me again. I'd make her."

"Love isn't made, it's a reflection. Without the light there's nothing to mirror. You don't love Nicole any more. It's all dead, finished."

"I love her to distraction—"

"Yes, you do, and you did, and in that distraction your mind lost its rightful theme. You had to kill a man to feed the love with vengeance. It all went wrong from there."

Half a minute ebbed, then:

"What will you do?"

"Simply what I must. I've no choice."

"But you alone know."

"I'm sorry, I can't forget murder."

"Why did you meddle? Why?"

"To help someone—"

"Nicole? My wife?"

"Of course."

"Better had she been left alone—"

"To go on submitting to the mental sadism that you inflicted. At least I'm human."

"Bishop, how much do you know of this?"

"Only a little. Enough."

"But not enough to convince the police they have a case . . . You came here to-night to force a confession from me, in some way or another—to find out where Trafford has gone . . ."

"Yes."

"And you know nothing; you simply suspect."

"The little that I know is all I need to know; and there is a witness of some facts of it. Remove me from your way, and there's still Helen—remove her too, and there's the one in Tallow Lane—too many to deal with."

The brown eyes blazed, became golden-flecked in a blade of reflected sunlight, that stabbed across from a picture-glass that mirrored the dying day. A vein rose against the pallid brow, and throbbed there, embossed by rage. It was the fear-ferocity of the trapped creature that now drove the man's beleaguered mind to thoughts of defence, escape, a way free.

"Pedley, you're finished, quite finished. You must realise it. Don't struggle like that, it only serves to make the end unpleasant."

Bishop was standing up, looking downwards at the poet in the cage. It was a scene almost intolerable in its implications; here sat a man already dead, with a mind that was designed only for artistry; what genius burned in it was now to blaze out, and it was going to be missed; there were too many in the world creating faster aeroplanes and deadlier weapons, too few whose task it was to provide the antidote, fine art. Soon there would be one fewer.

"Pedley, I'm going now."

"Sit down again."

"There's nothing more to be said—"

"No, but stay a little time. Sit down. We shall have a drink together."

The bulk of the man rose from the other chair: and Bishop did as he was asked. Pedley crossed the room, his feet shuffling a little on the thick pile like a tired man's, his shoulders lying forward in the white linen jacket like an older man's. In ten minutes, Harrison Pedley had aged ten years, and wanted a drink.

Bishop leaned back in the deep chair, his head tilted to the cushion, his eyes playing over the wall that faced him. On the wall was a trellis of shadow, thrown by the sun's last rays that slanted against the leaded windows. To the trellis there clung a single shadow-rose. Outside the windows, Bishop knew, the rose would be a living crimson flame, or perhaps a yellow bloom bright as a harvest-star, perhaps whiter than a winter's moon, perhaps shell-pink with coral's hue. But whatever its colour, only its soft grey ghost had passed through the leaded glass, and bloomed upon the wall, scentless and already dying, for it could not outlive the sun like the one outside.

Behind his chair, glass clinked, and liquid ran musically; and beneath these sharper sounds there came the heavy breathing of his host.

His voice broke into the breathing, but Bishop did not turn his head.

"It is to be Benedictine."

"Amen to that."

"Good. It's a drink fit for the sunset hour."

Against the wall the great shadow moved, blotting to death the trellis and the rose; and Bishop looked up and saw the wide white hand that was reaching down to him. In it was the diminutive glass, brimmed with the amber glow of the liqueur.

"Thank you."

When Pedley sank into the other chair, there sank with him all the violence of Trafford's end, hate and the jealousy that had been its cause, and the horror that had reigned after the act was made. All was drained, and Bishop saw an old man sitting down, a drink in his hand, and hopelessness in his heart.

The man had come out of a madness, and was tired of it and of life.

"I can think of nothing for a toast, my dear Bishop."

Bishop raised his glass.

"To Harrison Pedley, first producer on the London stage."

The plump shoulders shrugged.

"To him, if you will. To me."

The clock ticked, adding a sly, cynical comment.

The amber lay lower in the two glasses. Bishop said:

"Why did you ask me to stay?"

"For company, I think. It may be you've longer to live than I; life has become a niggardly measurement."

"You are innocent, as yet."

"Until proven guilty, yes. But I've no hopes."

He looked directly at his guest, and added quietly:

"I wish you had come to-morrow, instead; I wish you had done that. Just one day more, after so many..."

"It had occurred to me."

"But you wouldn't take the risk?"

"Not quite that. Call me a hypocrite if you will, but I came to-night out of kindness."

"To me?"

"Yes."

"You work in strange ways, my dear Bishop."

"Let me explain. To-morrow you produce *Othello*; perhaps the greatest *Othello* that London will ever have seen; if not the greatest, a very good one. You'll have ovation, no matter what else happens; your work on the play will ensure knowledge of what must happen next, you'll be cut off on the crest of triumph, the day after."

After a moment, softly:

"There are lesser deaths."

"That one is less than the one I can offer you. In any case we shouldn't mention death. This is England, and if its justice is not infallible, it's fairer than anywhere else. Your lawyer will be a brilliant man; your defence may possess—"

"I'm little interested in trials, Bishop. We were talking of my play."

"Very well. My point is this. If I'd waited until after the first night, I should have destroyed all the triumph of it. The first night is just a first step, I know that; afterwards comes work almost as hard as the rehearsals, until the play has a polish and a power that cannot be bettered whatever the producer does. You'd have launched a ship, and the captain would have stayed on shore. I didn't want that to happen; you don't deserve it, nor does London."

In the steady gaze of Pedley there was a light of expression that had nothing to do with anger or despair, fear or frustration; it was something near to hope.

"Go on, if you will, Bishop."

"There's not much more. I thought you should produce your play without the things in your mind that have been there for days and nights—the memory of murder, the subterfuge and the secrecy, the vile ecstasy that your hurting of Nicole brings. To-morrow night your mind ought to be freed of all that. In its place you must realise that this first night may well be your last. You've the chance to launch your ship with such magnificence that the crew can carry on. I think you can do that; I think you'll want to; I think you'll agree that it's the lesser of evils. It's the most I can offer. I'm sorry."

The room waited. A fragile skein of smoke climbed from the *meerschaum* bowl; the surface of the liqueur was placid in the glass; the little crimson archer held his bow with a muted tension as if awaiting the command to release.

"You offer much. You mean I am free to produce *Othello*, to-morrow night?"

"If you wish."

"I do. More than anything, I do. But meanwhile—?"

"Meanwhile I shan't trouble you."

"But I shall be watched—"

"No. You'll be completely free."

"Why do you trust me?"

"Because your easiest chance of escape has come and gone; and you didn't take it."

Pedley smiled faintly, remembering.

"I didn't take it, no . . . but I think I almost did. It was so easy. Only you know about me, and if I had removed you from my way, I could have dealt with the others, Helen and Robert Thorpe in Tallow Lane. You know little, but they know less." The smile died, and the white brow puckered, half in surprise. "I almost took my chance; what stayed my hand I don't quite know."

"Perhaps there was nothing heavy near enough—"

"Oh, yes—" the plump hand lifted, pointing to the sideboard where he had poured the drinks—"you can see it wasn't that."

Bishop turned his head, and saw the two silver candlesticks that stood there, slim against the sombre timber, their bases weighted.

"The nearer of those would have done," said Pedley quietly. "I looked at your head, that was resting against the cushion, and I thought of the nearer candlestick. It was something else that stopped me; perhaps the knowledge that it wasn't really a way out. Yet it would have been so simple, wouldn't it . . . I wonder that you trusted me, it so nearly happened."

"I didn't trust you. Sorry, but I couldn't expose myself deliberately—"

"But you were defenceless. I'd have made no sound behind you!"

"But had you raised the candlestick, its shadow

would have lifted against the wall."

Pedley turned his head, and the faint smile came again. He nodded.

"I see. Where the grey rose blooms."

"Yes. I sat watching it."

"I'm glad, of course. One cannot make a habit of madness without going off one's head..." He looked directly at Bishop again, and his voice was stronger and more confident. "I've come through weird country, Bishop. The first shock of awareness, the dreadful hurt, the uprooting of familiar joys whose roots are suddenly seen to be decayed ...and then the chance, and the blinding impulse ...and the act. Queer country, made up of heights and depths instead of woods and fields."

Bishop said, "The impulse and the act are the least important. It was what you did afterwards, to her. That's where the roots are rotten."

"I know...I know. And now they're ripped, and she can go free. I did no lasting harm; a little of anguish, a little of bewilderment, and maybe a broken heart. A girl's vicissitudes..."

"A child's, if you like, but to a child no less terrible. You had her on a rack."

Pedley nodded slowly, and there was no defiance or defence when he said, "Yes, I know. Then you came, and the day's work's done. Where is she now?"

"She's gone away."

The brown eyes brooded, widened to recent memories, narrowed to a little pain, and then resigned their gaze to emptiness.

"I'll never see her again."

"You'll see her often, but for the moment she's gone away."

"It wouldn't be safe for her in this house...now. I might extend my plans to further death, m'm? You're right, I might, if she came back. At this moment, nothing is further from my thoughts, but if I woke to a silent midnight, and remembered, and heard her soft breathing beside me in the room..."

"*Be thus when thou art dead...*"

"*And I will kill thee, and love thee after...*Yes, you were wise in seeing that she went away. Does she know everything?"

"Only that Trafford is dead."

"Whom does she suspect?"

"She's given it no thought; the fact's enough."

"She is in despair?"

"Not quite that. She's tired of it all, that's understandable. Pedley, why did you do it? I don't mean Trafford's death, but the other that came afterwards, the complex web of things—?"

"I'll bargain with you, Bishop. Tell me first how you found me out; then I'll tell you the other."

For a while Bishop was silent, thinking over the days of the week that was just ending. Last Friday he had met Nicole for the first time; to-day was

Thursday, and he was seeing her husband for the last. It had been a strange week; it was a strange week-end.

"I found you out," he said at last, "by adding together a lot of things that in a court of law would hold no more water than an upturned bowl. That gave me enough to think of you; but it wasn't conclusive until yesterday, at one o'clock. Then I met you face to face, and later realised whose face it was: a murderer's."

Pedley was watching him, the half-drunk liqueur in his right hand. His left hand had, a moment ago, knocked the red Knight to the carpet, accidentally, and the arm of the chair was vacant of the tiny archer and his shaft. Neither man had noticed. Bishop said:

"Until I went to the Honey Pot, I was working on nothing better than conjecture. But in Gerrard Street I found the key. The facts were figures, and there could be only one combination that would work. The facts were these: someone was blackmailing your wife. He was either Trafford or another. He had deliberately invited her to meet him at the Honey Pot, after she had said, in a letter, that she must see him."

Pedley's breathing was slow, as if he were almost waiting for Bishop to trip, to make a fault in his careful sequence of accusation.

"But Trafford never went to the Honey Pot. I

watched for him. He didn't go there before you went down the steps with Nicole; he was not in there when I joined you at the table; and it wasn't he who went there ten or fifteen minutes after we had left, because I called there later and showed them Trafford's photograph; they said the man who called for the note was different, without any doubt at all. So Trafford never kept the appointment; it wasn't he who had sent the invitation, it wasn't he who was writing to Nicole from Tallow Lane. I had never thought for one moment it was: it was too implausible. This confirmed it. So the blackmailer had sent the invitation. Why? He couldn't keep such an appointment, or the game would end. Then why make it? To persuade Nicole that Trafford still lived, and was near? But in not showing up, he was indicating the opposite. Am I near the truth?"

Pedley did not mope. His tone was gentle.

"You are indeed."

"I may go on?"

"If you will."

"Then the appointment must have been made for one purpose only: to be kept. The man who was torturing your wife in his subtle ways was there at the Honey Pot, at one o'clock. Again, for what purpose? Only one. To witness her anguish. To watch her, cat-and-mouse, while she sat, distraught and concealing the fear she felt, as she waited for Trafford to appear, as she waited—her mind torn and

divided in balanced agony—hoping desperately
that the boy would come, so that she could just have
sight of him and be assured he lived and was well
and still perhaps loved her—and hoping desperately that he would *not* come, because you sat there
in his place ... A torture, Pedley, so exquisite that
it could have been conceived of only by a poet inspired by hate. A situation so subtle and so dramatic
that only the most superb production of the scene
could bring it to life. Where else had I to look? The
appointment had been kept; the scene was played
most sensitively, and took its place with all honours
among the other scenes that go to make this play
of yours ... the one you have told us you are writing
now."

He got up quietly from his chair, and with a
matchstick cleared the dottle from his pipe, into
the ashbowl in the hearth. As he turned to face the
room again, Pedley looked up at him with a strange
gaze that for a moment was impossible to interpret;
then the puckish smile came to the fleshy mouth,
and Pedley raised his liqueur-glass.

"To the most appreciative critic I have ever had,"
he said. Bishop took his own unfinished drink. Re-
calling the earlier toast and its acknowledgement
he said:

"To him, if you will. To me."

The Benedictine was drained, and Pedley too
stood up.

"I made a bargain, Bishop. You've told me how you found me out; I'll tell you how I came to do the thing I did—but not at once. Will to-morrow be too too late?"

He was crossing to the desk, where the ivory pieces stood in their red and white array. The key turned, the drawer slid out, and he laid the book on the crimson-leathered flap. Bishop had made no answer; Pedley went on: "I can tell you best, you see, by giving you this book. It is of course my... play. Written, as I think I mentioned, in the form of a diary."

His plump hand turned the pages casually, the deep brown eyes selecting briefly passages of the careful handwriting. The thick cream paper scuffed harshly in the silent room.

"When, to-morrow?" Bishop asked. "I mean what time?"

Pedley looked up, closing the book.

"In the afternoon, would that suit you? A few hours, shall we say, before my first night, and my last. My reason is obvious. The Devil has, after all, given me the third Act of my play... and I must set it down."

"I understand."

"I think I said, my dear Bishop, that if the third Act did not come to my mind, I would trade my soul with him for it—and ten per cent of the gross receipts." He stood slackly at the desk, his knuckles resting on the leather flap. "Unfortunately my soul is not enough, nor ten per cent of anything in the world. There is nothing, I believe, with which I can strike a bargain."

The tone made it a statement; but the question was clear enough. Bishop began fitting the chess-pieces into the oblong box. Not looking at Pedley he said softly:

"Nothing. I wish there were."

"So be it. Let me help you re-pack these exquisite things."

The two men handled them, placing them carefully into the box, not speaking, as if they were putting together the fragments of something broken by mischance; but Bishop's answer still echoed in the room, though the words were gone. There was nothing that could make the fragments whole again, nothing at all in the world.

"There."

"Thank you, sir. Now I must go."

"You must, Mr. Bishop. You've stayed almost my lifetime; I'm sorry it could not be longer."

"I share that feeling."

At the door of the car, Pedley laid a hand on the other's arm. "If—you see her, say something kind from me. I leave the choice to you."

Bishop nodded, sitting behind the wheel.

"I will."

He looked for a little time—perhaps a second,

maybe more—into the deep brown eyes. They were not hurt, nor reproachful; pity was in them, that was all. Bishop said:

"One thing I'd like to be assured of. There'll be a production of *Othello*, to-morrow night?"

Pedley stood back from the car, framed against the massed ivy and the vacant windows.

"There will be a production of *Othello* to-morrow night. One of the finest London has ever seen." He lifted his head, and a harshness came into his voice. "Good night, Mr. Bishop. I'm sorry you came."

"Then you'll be glad to see me go. Good night."

The grey saloon slid phantom-like along the curving drive; and then its lean form met the gates, and vanished through them.

For minutes Pedley remained by the porch, where the strands of honeysuckle twined about the columns and clematis clung; then he turned, and went into his empty house, moving slowly and in some puzzlement as if he had come to answer the door, but had found that no one was there.

14th

MOVE

BISHOP WENT INTO GRAY'S HOTEL at ten o'clock the same evening and was shown up to Mrs. Pedley's suite. The page retired.

"I'm sorry about that."

She was a little cool. "You find me quite obedient; there's no call for regret."

"I had no choice. You had to be made to leave the house and this was the best way—"

"It was merely to get me away from the house? Why?"

Coolness had gone; anxiety came.

"For no reason that's very sensational. I wanted to talk to Harrison." He picked up a petal, fallen from one of the three amber roses that were poised in a vase, and rolled it between his fingers.

"It must have been a serious talk, Hugo."

From the petal moisture bled between his fin-gertips.

"Yes. But everything's quite all right now."

He took swift stock of her mood and decided to go on. "Harrison would rather not see you again for a day or two, just as you'd rather not see him. It's very simple. You don't mind staying here for those few days?"

"I must know why." The green eyes were wary; much of the lassitude that had been her reaction to the news of Trafford's death was slipping from her; and she was almost alert again; she cared, about several things.

"I can't tell you why, exactly. I can tell you ... on Saturday—"

"Saturday is important, isn't it? It keeps coming up."

"It does, doesn't it. Will you wait until then?"

"I expect I'll have to, unless I phone Harrison."

Bishop dropped the shrivelled remains of the petal and came closer to her. "I wish you wouldn't," he said.

"I won't, but please tell me just a little more."

"All right. He and I talked about Trafford. He knew about Trafford already."

She drew a quick little breath.

"How long has he known?"

"A long time."

"Before I met you?"

"As far as I know, two weeks before then; it may have been longer."

She turned away and looked out of the window, down through the flimsy net to where the lights burned in the street. They still crowded the sun's death-bed, watchful and unwinking. She looked very small against the window, slim in silhouette. Her slight body was a little slack, a little tired. She murmured:

"Poor Harrison."

Bishop used Pedley's own words of a little while ago.

"Save your pity."

"I'm a woman, and it's been my fault. What's Harrison going to do?"

"Produce a brilliant *Othello* to-morrow night. Nicole, I managed to get a box. Vera Gorringe is going with me. Would you sit with us?"

As she turned the street's glow was cast across her face; a very young face, that of a child with a broken doll in her hands.

"Thank you," she said.

"And afterwards, on Saturday, you'll go away, for a few days?"

"I could stay here—"

"No, somewhere right out of London. It's too hot, in London, too sticky. Everyone gets jaded here in this weather."

"All right, I'll go away. To Hampshire. Would Hampshire do?"

"Nicely. Until then, have you sent for your things?"

She nodded. "A week-end case."

He was by the door. "You can always send for more, if you decide to stay away a bit longer. Do it through me, I'll fix it up. Now I must go."

She came towards him from the window, and he accepted the two small hands in his.

"Hugo, I know something's happened, I mean something more than that Harrison has known about me for weeks. But I don't think I want to find out just what it is. Do you think that's right?"

"Very right."

"Then I won't try to work it all out. You say that everything's over. How much ought I to thank you?"

"Judge for yourself, when you know everything. I'll be lucky, then, to hear even one word of thanks." He pressed the small cool hands and took away his own, and opened the door. "If you get bored, Nicole, you know my number; but try all your friends first, you'll find them less oyster-like. Good night, my dear."

He was halfway towards the lift when he heard her door close; and now, as if he realised he was no longer within sight, he let himself think of her. Trafford must have loved her very much. He must have loved her more than any of his others, and if that might not have been very deeply, it had been the most he was able.

One day she would find a man who was not years older than she and did not possess a mind too civilised for simple passions; a man who was not an over-passionate young troubadour whose mere looks had a price too high. Between two such men she had fallen; later she would find her balance, and she had all the time in the world.

"Down, sir?"

Bishop's eyes widened.

"M'm?"

"Going down, sir?"

"Yes. Please. Going down."

The gates clattered shut discordantly, like a chime on a broken bell.

The red wax cracked, tearing the paper, powdering away from the string.

"I also suggested that she should share our box to-night. Do you mind?"

"Of course not."

"Your enthusiasm is slightly less than burning."

"Dear Hugo, you witness a woman in torment. Until you choose to tell me what's happened I'm going out. I can bear so much of your sensational silence, but not without limit."

The stiff brown paper unfolded; and the book was revealed. Bishop leaned back in his chair and looked at the book and said:

"I'm about to do so much talking that you may be bored before I'm finished. But I don't think so."

Vera Gorringe swung round from the door.

"This is it?"

He nodded. "This is it. I should make yourself comfortable."

The late-afternoon sunlight streamed across his shoulders, and the clear-cut shadow of the telephone flew across the desk as he picked it up.

"Mr. Willing, no callers, please, for the next two hours. With two exceptions: Mr. or Mrs. Harrison Pedley. Yes. Thank you."

His forefinger began dialling. Miss Gorringe said:

"Inspector Frisnay telephoned this morning. I left a note on your desk."

"Yes. His impatience is now about to increase, or diminish, according to how wise a man he is."

On a chair near the davenport, the Princess Chu Yi-Hsin sat up, and with one paw scratched an ear. Miss Gorringe said:

"Your Highness, please. You are not in Siam."

The lean fawn head swung, and the sapphire eyes regarded the woman.

"Inspector Frisnay? Bishop."

"About time. I phoned yesterday and this morning—"

"And now I'm on the same game. Ain't it a lark? Please listen."

"Well?"

"The Trafford case is closed. Will you meet me this evening at about ten?"

"You can't just ring up and say the case is closed. Come round here now and—"

"I hate to cut in, Freddie, but I've a lot to do. I'll be at the Parthenon Theatre at ten o'clock or at the curtain, whichever is the earlier. If you meet me there, you can have the whole issue."

"Is this absolutely Lloyd's, Hugo?"

"A.1. I guarantee it. You can be quite assured I'm not letting you down."

After a long pause Frisnay said:

"All right, I'm going to accept that."

"Good. Meantime, will you stop enquiries?"

"Not officially. I can't."

"I know. But off the record. I'm not just playing you up. It might easily save you an awful lot of work later if you let me keep things under control until ten this evening. I think that."

"Very well. Enquiries will continue: officially."

"Fair do's. Would you be outside Box D on curtain-down? Don't go in, I'll explain why when we meet."

"Outside Box D, Parthenon, ten or end-of-show."

"Till then."

"Till then."

The receiver dropped gently into its cradle.

Bishop lifted the lid from the tobacco-bowl, and filled his pipe very slowly and carefully. His fingers were not steady, because in front of him was the heavy leather-bound book, and to open it would be like switching on the light in an unknown room, or topping the brow of the hill in a strange country. A secret lay on the sunlit desk, and in a moment it would break.

The match cursed harshly across the box, and the flame challenged the sunshine and lost, content to raise a scowl of blue-grey smoke from the pipe's bowl. Then the spent match died bitterly in the ash-tray, and the smoke died away in frail skeins.

"Ready?" he murmured.

Vera Gorringe nodded.

"Yes."

He opened the book.

15th

MOVE

BISHOP BEGAN READING.
Vera Gorringe listened.
The cat slept in the chair.

FRIDAY, JUNE 6th

I am not sure what to do.

I am not even sure that it is true; but I think it must be. I am so desperate to believe it false that I must make a choice: my heart breaks or I encage myself in a Paradise where only a fool would go. So I believe it is true, that what I have heard, quite by chance and with a shock sublime, is not a filthy tale but news of simple fact.

But she has shown nothing; or I concentrate too hard on work and observe nothing. I dare not ask her, in case she denies it. I could bear admission, but not a lie. So I must wait. I shall not record even his name in this hideous journal whose pure pages I would like to rip and rend even as I turn them, would like to burn and watch them shrivel in a blaze. I shall leave out his name, until I am sure; and, if I am sure it is true, his name shall go down here in its uncouth little syllables; if I find it is false—oh, God, for that gift above all!—the name need not go down. I shall merely watch the blaze of the ripped pages while my anger burns away; then I must go to her and ask if she will forgive me for my doubts.

She would forgive me, for their foundation is firm. A friend told me, for my sake. For my sake! What saved me from killing my friend when he did me this appalling kindness? I am not sure. I am not sure of anything; least of all you, my dear love.

FRIDAY, JUNE 13th
Yes, such a day and date, and I am sure.

For convenience we measure a week in seven single days; the last week ran to a hundred years, and I am an old man now. There has come an end to matters, and it finds me half-naked by a morning stream like a sated satyr who wakes to remember only a lonely dream.

I am sure now of it, but still not sure of what to do. That will come to me in a little while. I have my work, and that must keep me sane. In three weeks from to-day I have *Othello* for my Parthenon. It will open, and it will be a good play, if the producer has not by then become himself the Moor. But that would be absurd. My death is not worth the murder of a whore.

SUNDAY, JUNE 15th, EVENING

Strange that, thinking in this hellish book of making a murder, I should have made it so soon. No strangeness of course in that, but in its being of him and not of her.

Trafford, his name. Deceased.

The matter was not complicated. I had laid no plans. The boy simply came to me, to talk to me. To ask me—and such was his monstrous impudence—if I would divorce my wife...We spoke frankly, in accordance with our subject. During the conversation he suggested that I was too old to love my wife in the manner she desired. He also was good enough to remark that I now inspired in her not the smallest spark of passion.

Then I killed him and he said nothing more.

If there was no passion in me, the fates must have lent me one brief storm, for the boy was dead at my feet and I was breathing heavily. I throttled him, I think, for there was no blood nor any instrument, and the young face was mottled and aghast. And my rage was done. It had died with the little wagging tongue that had dared to utter things that concerned my love and me and no other; least of all a strutting trouper's brat.

I placed the remains aside, where they would not obtrude upon the pleasant scene of house and garden, and then I thought of Nicole. My mind, having dealt with the lusty buck, turned to view his strumpet; and the rage came back.

To-day is Sunday and the boy is gone; but she shall know a week of agonies, a month of misery. She shall walk in nightmare through the days, and when she comes to the dawn she'll find it midnight still.

To-day is Sunday, and more has already come to the matter than my day's good deed. Soon after I had placed the cadaver where its presence could foul neither eye nor nose, my telephone summoned me. Janet, the girl, said that it was a lady who had not given her name. When I went to the telephone I heard the voice of Helen Ledine. We had seldom met; our spheres were a little distant.

I will record what I recall of the conversation.

"Mr. Pedley, forgive my phoning you, but I wondered if you could tell me where Mr. Trafford is."

Something of a shock claimed me. The boy's blood was scarcely chilled, yet here was an enquirer. And I realised consciously and for the first time that I was technically a murderer.

"Mr. Trafford?"

"Yes. Roy Trafford. He told me he was going to see you."

And for the first time I realised also that I must take steps to avoid the technical consequences. I had no mood on me to die. The world had work for me.

"Indeed? I may be able to help you, Miss Ledine. You are in town?"

"Yes, I am."

The voice sounded a little upon guard; but the necessity for that could not have been greater than mine.

"I wonder, then, if you would give me the pleasure of dining with you this evening?"

Puzzled; yes, she was puzzled. That was good.

"I should—like that."

"Excellent." We made our plans to meet, and the unsettling conversation ceased. I was much troubled by it, for it opened the doors to unconsidered things: the Ledine girl had been told that Trafford was seeing me to-day. Who else knew? Did Nicole?

If many knew, I would be exposed to great danger. If only one, or two, there might be hope of investing the matter with silence, for all time. If only Ledine, then I could deal with her. If Nicole also . . . already there were plans in my clearing head that would convince my Nicole that the boy still lived.

———

We dined in a quiet place selected by myself. The meal was not unpleasant in any aspect; certainly the challenge that had sprung from Trafford's death was to my mind a sudden stimulation. Forces now opposed my will; and all of my life my will has developed to the theme of opposition. Challenge has always been the fire in which the strength in me is forged. Now more than ever.

"He told you that he was to see me to-day?"

She nodded, watching me closely. I said to her: "When did he tell you this?"

"This morning."

"He mentioned the business we were to discuss?"

"May I speak frankly?"

"To do less would waste our time."

"All right. He said he was going to ask you to—divorce Mrs. Pedley."

"Ah. A somewhat singular suggestion, coming from a stranger."

She did not disguise her contempt for my presence.

"Mr. Pedley, in case you wonder what this business is of mine, I should tell you that Roy Trafford and I are—together."

"I see."

"I expect you do. I expect he mentioned it to you."

"Had he talked to me to-day, he might well have mentioned it and sundry other things; as he failed to visit me, the opportunity was lost. However, I hope you will remain—er—together; your art is similar, and both employ it well. It seems a happy circumstance."

For a while she said nothing. I had taken the first step and made my first denial. But the next was dangerous, a tacit admission. I placed all my faith in it.

"My dear, we appear to have dealt with the question of Trafford. I'm sorry he did not come to see me; he is an interesting young man and should one day make his name on the London stage. I am grateful to him, however, for having persuaded you—unwittingly—to telephone me; because I have considered such a meeting as this for some while. I am interested in your career, no less than in his."

She maintained her silence, and I was glad. If I had the power I would replace her tawdry little lover with an offer of success. Helen Ledine, as she was now, might be my most dangerous opponent; but I could make an actress of her, and a friend.

"I would like," I told her, "to develop your talent."

She eyed me with a serious gaze, and I knew what was in her mind. As a producer I had achieved much; my name was high. I could change the life of a woman such as she, by uttering a word. I had already spoken it.

"I'm very interested," she said.

"Of course. The chance is rare. Who is your agent?"

"Harry Bond."

"A good man, but too small for you. A manager must be found; I have one. But this is business, and it is Sunday night. Perhaps if you'd meet me again in more appropriate environment—my office, to-morrow, say..."

She knew. It was too obvious to escape her notice. But she tested it.

"I'd welcome that. I'd be unwise not to appreciate what you're offering. There is, I imagine, no part for Roy Trafford in your plans?"

"Unhappily, no. The boy has promise, but his work during the last year has impressed me less than yours. There is, I fear, no part...whatsoever ...in my plans."

"I understand."

"I wonder."

"You can be sure."

And that was all. Our discussion might have followed slightly different lines; it occupied certainly longer than two hours; but these were the bones of it. She did not know—she could scarcely know—that night the real reason for my unexpected offer. She realised simply that I had no interest in Trafford, nor in his alleged visit; she realised that was a condition of business. I was satisfied.

Later, when the boy is missed, she will realise more; and I believe the treasure I tendered in my hand for her to take will prove of greater value than she would draw from other means; it would not gain her much to say the world that Trafford was to visit me to-day. It will gain her much to forget it. I can make her name, and, if there is any art in the girl, I will. Otherwise she could be my death.

Nicole has not returned yet. She said she would be back tomorrow morning, Monday. She left before lunch to-day, to visit a friend. I wonder . . . for it was a sudden plan. This morning, quite early, the telephone rang, and it was for her. Hermione Webster had been trying to get in touch with her and had failed until now. Would she stay the day, and night, in Hampshire?

But I wonder. Was it Trafford who telephoned, asking her to go away for a little time, so that the two men could work their twin wills one upon the other?

If so, the one was too feeble; the other much too rash. Already I feel regret, because this will disturb my concentration upon *Othello*.

I am rather tired. On the day of rest I have done dread work, and my wife is still a carnal wench, and not the goddess I knew. I will go to bed, for the first time utterly alone.

WEDNESDAY, JUNE 18th

To-day I have seen Robert Thorpe. He is little changed, as friendly and as loyal. I am still sorry I was unable to keep him in my employ; on the other hand he has set up a good little business with the slight reward I gave him those years ago. His shop in Tallow Lane is flourishing, and I was happy to see him there among his wallflowers and sweet-peas.

He has agreed to receive letters there for the name of Trafford. I merely implied that the matter was not weighty but delicate, and told him that if he would prefer my finding another address he must say that. He said that it was a small thing to do for me after what he called his treatment while in my employ. I was quite touched; he is a courteous fellow and not of these times.

I also told him that it was possible a lady would call, asking for this Mr. Trafford (I did not say it was my wife; Thorpe has never met my Nicole). If she called, I asked him, would he give her a message?

He assured me that he would, and I am amused.

If she goes there, and my message is given, she will not understand a word of it; nor will Robert Thorpe; yet it will delight me to know, later, if the message was ever given and received. Because only I in the world know its meaning. I and one other. What a pity she will not understand!

FRIDAY, JUNE 20th

I wrote to my wife to-day. I typed it, as the poor boy used to do. In a box-room of the theatre there is an old machine, once used as a property and still quite manageable. I wrote:

Dear one,

Please try to understand so many things; my absence, my silence until now, and the thing I have to ask. I am well, though harassed; I can't get back for a while, though I'd dare a million deaths to talk to you again ...to hold you and hear you say my name.

For a reason too involved to explain, I am desperate for money. It is not a debt, or any sordid mess I find myself in; but it concerns our future, and it is part of the plans I said I'd make when we last saw each other. Please trust me, and believe me when I say that you wouldn't hesitate if you knew my reasons. I need two hundred pounds. Sorry to have to come down to it so crudely, but I'm not able to write a decently long letter yet.

I have no other resources. If you can't manage it, I shall have to throw everything to the winds, and ask your husband. That, as you can imagine, is the last thing I want to do.

Forgive my haste, and try to remember only that I love you.

Roy.

A strange letter, from a lover; but I think the wording is right. There has to be created a sense of balance, and this is it.

I wonder if there'll be an answer, from my wife?

SATURDAY, JUNE 21st

I am almost happy that I began it all. With each day's progress in the matter is offered a new subtlety for my palate. For example:

This morning she received the letter, and this very evening she came to me, and asked for a cheque for her account. It was all I could do not to tell her that it was quite unnecessary. But I gave it to her, without a question. It was not a large sum, and it pleased me to hear her thanks. I looked at her, and admired how sweet she seemed, how soft of voice, and wide of eye, how young and maidenly she posed beside my desk as she asked her good husband for money to give her lover...It was at that moment that any pity in me for her died; and I am glad, freed of it.

The situation, of course, appeals to me greatly. If ever I make this comedy into a three-Act play, it will possess a sequence of the most piquant situations, such as the one that developed this evening: I am blackmailing my own wife, in her lover's name—and I am also affording her the funds... The cheque I have so generously signed to-night will return to me, through Tallow Lane...I doubt if blackmail was ever committed in such delicious circumstances. But then there's France in my blood; a true Britisher would look askance at such a sense of honour.

France, yes...my dear parents, turn you both in the grave you entered when I was scarcely five? Your little boy has grown up, *mes vieux*, to a monster's proportions! I am glad you do not know, but you would appreciate this play I am creating, and its delicate machinery. Look well:

Had I told her simply the boy was dead she would have broken her heart. She would have gone on loving him, however hopeless. Even when the love, too, had died, she would have remembered him softly and with a tear. That was not enough for me. I shall break her heart, and her love for the dead as well. Let her see how mercenary her gay young buck of a lover has become: his price is two hundred pounds...Let her realise another humiliation; the value of money that she has never had to know. Let her come to me for it, even her commodious conscience pricked at the thought of what she does. Until now, I have seen that there is nothing she lacks; it has been unnecessary for me to foster her account, for there have been few gifts I have not given on my own thought, and those few she has asked for, and received. Now let her find the want of money, to buy herself the secret that she keeps from me...Let her savour the thought that she is not only unfaithful to her good husband, but asks him for pelf to pay her seducer off...

But I must never tell her the cream of the jest: that it has no point, that every cheque I'll sign for her will return to me through Tallow Lane. She plies a treadmill that turns full-circle and nought accomplishes, but I must never let her know. That would spoil the game.

I wait with impatience for her reply to my letter of this morning. I know, at least, that it will contain the cheque, but with what message?

A message, I think, of less passion than she held for him before.

TUESDAY, JUNE 24th

Of much less passion, yes.

I will not record her words here, because passion has not completely died in her; and I shall not mimic endearments in my diary from her to another heart. A dead heart, already clotted with its own chill blood; but even so.

Her letter to him, enclosing his tawdry fee, is the story of my success. I read it avidly. Its words are warm still, yet cooler than they must have been before, when they had wantoned in word and deed beyond my sight. I am reading, and will be reading in her letters to him, of my own secret achievement. With the cooling of each sentiment I shall watch the effect of the letters "he" writes to her. I am breaking down their love; I play them as an instrument: and soon will come the final frantic discord, and what music was in them will cease.

It is a play of good ideas, a tragedy of passion, a comedy of situation. One day I must surely change the names and choose my cast. At present the play has no title, but I will find one. At present the play has audience of only one: its playwright and producer. Its leading lady, Nicole, fair of face and with a heart so young as to be quite without worth. Its leading man, Trafford...already dead—and there's a situation for a jaded critic! As dead as Hamlet's ghost, the boy struts on across my secret stage...

I am the producer, and our letters are the script. My wife for the lead, her lover opposite and speaking his lines (in my letters in his name) from the grave, which is my scenery. Surely even *Othello* has not the magic of this subtle fancy? I do not claim to have bettered the Bard; only to have alighted by chance upon a prettier plot...

Yet not a great deal prettier: there is in *Othello* much for thought, and these days I watch her face as she stares with me to the stage, and I know what she is wondering. She wonders if I shall one night play the Moor to her guilty Desdemona. I see that in her face.

Let her wonder. There may come a time when it shall be revealed to her that far worse than that is going on.

To-day I shall acknowledge her letter.
One must be businesslike.

FRIDAY, JUNE 27th

To-day I talked to Helen; or she talked to me. She
is an interesting person, but not very intelligent. It
seems that upon that gruesome Sabbath morning,
Trafford declared to Helen his intention of coming
to see me; and the poor girl passed the rest of the
day praying that I should not be persuaded to divorce my wife! For if I did (I think Maurice Ducar-
tier once wrote a novel round this pretty situation),
then Helen would lose her young rake-hell . . . and it
would be a double divorce, morally speaking.

She was furious with her errant swain all that
day, and telephoned me in the afternoon because
she could wait no longer to hear the verdict; was
her lover's lover to be divorced from the husband,
or could dear Helen remain in possession of the
defeated paramour? (*"Fain would I climb, yet fear
I to fall . . ."*—well poor boy, you certainly climbed,
and I am sorry I had to press away your life by rule
of thumb.)

She has not asked me where Trafford is, or even
if I know. She's a good girl, little Ledine. I shall set
her among the heights if she remains as silent and
as untroublesome as now.

———

A week to the first night. I quake all day and some-times forget the other matter, and find myself gaz-ing at my wife as though I loved her. Soon I shall stop quaking and put the company through fire and brimstone, and we shall make a good play, and everyone will like it. But what a pity *Othello* lacks the subtler story of another piece! Perhaps I shall one day be known not as the London Producer but as the Man Who Wrote That Simply Delicious Play with the Gruesome Situations in it that were so Killingly Comic.

If I did not think of it as amusing, I should take my life, and where's the point in that? Oh, Nicole!

SATURDAY, JUNE 28th

A strange day; I feel that there are events in the making, matters on the march, forces assembling behind me. Conscience, of course, the onset of creeping guilt.

My dear wife has posted a letter to me to-day.

She came back to the house and there was noth-ing in her manner nor her eyes to tell me she had just sent a letter to her love. There was nothing in my manner nor my eyes to tell her that the letter would have come to me, that I was her true love and not a decaying cadaver.

She really believes what I am trying to make her

believe, that Trafford is blackmailing her—let us not bandy euphemisms in this book. Of course the boy was in debt, as all know; but what she did not know was the measure of his mercenary soul. She is beginning to know him, through me. It is a false picture, but then so is the one I once had of her; the sweet and gentle wife, the brilliant critic of my brilliant work.

I am impatient to read what she had written to me to-day, to him that is to say. In the seeming madness of my theme there is much sound practicality:

Letter by letter she will realise that her ardent young lover is a very cool-headed man. She will— rather than come to me to confess—come to me to ask for what he demands. I shall of course give without stint or question, and she will feel worse for that. Harried by a blackmailer, she will see her good husband emerge as kindly and generous, in contrast with the passionate paramour who took her body and soul and then demanded payment for his pleasures. This is not clever of me. It is simple logic, practically applied. I am producing my play, as always, with a modest intelligence.

Only one thing worries me a little to-day. She had a letter this morning from Trafford; it asked for fifty pounds. Her reply was posted this evening; I watched her sweet slim figure through the gates: but she has not asked me to-day for another cheque. Am I forcing the poor girl too hard?

To-night, as I was writing the above, the telephone summoned me and offered the voice of Helen. She has passed an hour with a certain Mr. Bishop. Now who is he? She assures me that he is not connected with the law, yet he appears to be trying to find Trafford. He is dangerous, dear Helen said also, to me.

Is there another character impatient to enter my new play? It sometimes happens: one designs the plot, and begins writing, only to find that a new character will help the action or the theme. Such characters are often persistent, and one has to make a place for them.

But where shall I put my Bishop? I must consider him, and his unexpected claim.

A note on Characterisation, I think, is fitting here.

NICOLE PEDLEY: Young, naïve enough to consider herself sophisticated; married to a man fifteen years her senior. Finds herself caught up in a drama of her own foolish making.

HARRISON PEDLEY: Her husband, a producer. Of French parentage, brought up in England from the age of five, when his parents were killed in an accident. This uprooting, at a crucial age, partly accounts for emotional instability. Jealous of his young wife, and—it comes to light—not without cause. (Let us face the naked facts): His pride lacerated by her infidelity, he chooses a means of revenge based upon crude murder—the *crime passionel*—but built with more delicate and subtle architecture.

ROY TRAFFORD: Young, ardent, not intelligent but physically attractive in an animal fashion; the typical cavalier whose godly head is a mere shell of creature themes.

MR. BISHIP: Who is he, and where is his place?

HELEN LEDINE: A fair actress of whose talent something might be made. Prepared to forget her lover for the sake of such an offer from a leading figure in the London Theatre, even though she must suspect it is a bribe. She knows she has lost the boy in any case: he is now engaged upon seducing a greater lady; so Helen decides to cut her losses, and, in the loss of Trafford, is prepared to gain a much more glittering treasure: her name as a London actress of high stature.

ROBERT THORPE: A little pawn. A good, loyal, honest little pawn.

So much for Characterisation. In brief:

    NICOLE: victim of Harrison Pedley.
    HARRISON: victim of Nicole Pedley.
    TRAFFORD: victim of circumstance.
    HELEN: the most fortunate person in the play.

But my Muse is my wife, and she whispered evil to my ear, unknowing. I am the victim of all evil, but, like a good mirror, I reflect it back. That is justice.

TUESDAY, JULY 1st
   I have her letter, the one that was posted on the evening of Saturday. It was brief. I opened it this morning, in the little box-room at the theatre. It said:

> Roy,
>   I must see you.
>   N.

For some minutes I sat thinking. There was no direct sunlight in the room, but radiance flowed through the windows from the face of the buildings across the street. When I had finished thinking, I slipped a sheet of notepaper into the Steinrohl typewriter, and replied to the letter. The message was as brief, but she will understand.

I was a little annoyed with her. There had been

no cheque, either with her own signature or mine. But I am fair enough to blame myself partly for this. I should have asked less than two hundred pounds in the first instance, and more than fifty pounds in the second. I am not used to this sort of thing. One must obey certain natural laws, certain demands on simple psychology. First, fifty, then perhaps seventy-five; then a hundred: and so on. It is much more reasonable. The screw must turn gently, and slowly, not come down with a sudden twist and then release.

I tucked the letter into a plain white envelope that bore her typed name and address. Before this evening I posted it in South Kensington, so that the post-mark would be right.

The letter will make her happy, for a while. For a few hours she will know relief from wretchedness. I have allowed her that, in the few words of my reply. I felt a most saintly man as I left the sunless room, and went down the flight of stairs, humming a tune....

———

I also booked a table to-day, for the meeting of Trafford and Nicole, to-morrow at the Honey Pot, at one o'clock. I booked it in Trafford's name. Why not?

WEDNESDAY, JULY 2nd
   A day full of fascination ... or let me give it a truer title: a day of self-satisfaction. Everything went

splendidly. At breakfast I knew that among her letters there was the one from "Trafford": the one I had written yesterday. The conversation was light and carefree, for she acted brilliantly:

"Lots of fun, Nicole?"

"M'm?"

"Gay invitations to the rightest parties?"

"Oh. Not quite. You remember Susan?"

"The girl with plaits?"

And so on; it was delicious. I had asked her if there were any invitations in her post: and even she did not realise how psychic I was, for she had not been able to open the letter...I rather enjoyed that; though perhaps it was a shade over-subtle; and this secret appreciation of such situations is becoming a lonely delight: one should share these things with a sympathetic audience. I shall, if ever I write this into a play and produce it. I hope I do, for it would be sad to waste such material.

We talked of other things—Gillison's coming up from Stratford for *Autumn Gold*—my sending Helen to Tony for the lead (poor Nicole, who could not tell me why she detests Ledine so!)—and then I think I paid her some slight compliment; and she thanked me, and said she was always a bore at breakfast. I kissed her hand for that. I did not kiss her face, because my lips would not have been Trafford's, and she would have longed for the earthy animal adolescence in their touch. But I kissed her hand that would soon (if only I would leave her!) rip open the love-letter that I had sent her in his name.

Poor boy, he cannot raise a hand to pen a word, for his fingers have beetles at their chilly tips.

I told her, just before we left the house, that this morning's work would be important; because I had to begin my little campaign whose simple aim was to bring her to the Honey Pot at one o'clock ... with me. For in so many ways I represent the dead.

Before she went from the breakfast-room she had a pang of guilt, perhaps of pity. It was amusing to watch, to hear:

"Thank you for—saying such nice things to me."

She stood by the door. Between us were the flowers on the table; we saw each other over the heads of yellow roses. I took the cigarette-holder slowly from my mouth, smiling to her, pretending a little surprise.

"Dear Nicole, you are such a nice person."

They may not have been our precise words; my memory is not infallible; but such was the sense of them. She opened the door; the duty was done, I could see. She had tried to make amends for all the deceit and the ugliness and the estrangement that had dwelled between us among the yellow blooms; but she must have known that if ever she wanted me back, she must do so much more than that.

When she came from the porch to the car where

I sat waiting there was in her walk a quickness, in her eyes a brightness; suddenly she was young at twenty-nine.

She had, of course, opened the letter.

This morning I completed my campaign. It was necessary for me to make her afraid of my mood, so that she would not dare to offer me an excuse at lunch-time. She knew this morning's work was vital; she knew I expected her verdict as a critic over the luncheon-table. I was not sure how I would arrange it that we went to the Honey Pot instead of to Green's, where we usually go; but something would occur.

This morning I gave the company hell. It did them no harm. We finished brilliantly. The rehearsals are going more than well.

And by lunch-time Nicole was in pieces, poor child. She had seen my mood, my anger; she knew that no excuse would suffice to take her away from our discussion of the work; she knew also that, at one o'clock, her dark-eyed Romeo would await her in Gerrard Street... For me it was an exciting moment; how would the heroine of my play react to this twist in the plot?

Less well than she might. When casting, I should perhaps design this particular character with more fire, more resourcefulness.

But the situation was sound, for all that. She played into my hands, complaining that the heat of the day distressed her.

"Harrison, I'm feeling—rather funny."

She passed a hand over her brow, not very well because she was only half-acting; the heat was indeed stifling. She tried, as a final desperate gesture:

"Could you let me have an hour's rest somewhere, I—"

I said, "My dear, of course!" for here was the answer to my little problem. In the Honey Pot—a basement—it would be cool. . . .

And there we drove, the wife, the husband, and the lover's ghost. (Suggest curtain here, possibly End of Scene. A good moment. Scene: entering Honey Pot.)

It was of course a delicious lunch. I knew not what I ate, but the fare was rich for my senses. Before joining me at the corner-table she managed to slip away, and leave a note for Trafford. (I have it here, now, as I write this page of my diary. I asked young Emmerson to run along to the restaurant within minutes of our returning to the theatre, and enquire if there were a note for a Mr. Trafford. There was, as I suspected.)

When she joined me at the table I was able to begin the scene. Its production was already designed; I merely guided it. She sat limply, poor lamb, her eyes torn to the entrance whenever people came in. At a centre table, Francesca had a party of friends; she screamed loudly at odd moments— a nice nerve-racking background to point my theme. (I must remember to bring in these incidental characters; they have a good place here.)

It was when a perfect stranger arrived that I was surprised. It was the old story of a new character popping up and claiming the playwright's attention. He came to our table, tall, quiet, a little too self-composed. He said simply:

"Well, well—Mrs. Pedley. How are you?"

I even thought he might really be an acquaintance. She offered him her hand lightly as I stood up. I give her this: her soft voice scarcely sounded a tremor.

"How nice to see you again!"

Then she introduced us, and we looked at each other. So this was Bishop. It will be interesting to discover where his place is in my play; but, despite my confidence in myself as supreme producer, I somehow fear the man.

I must surmount that odd feeling. He is merely a new character, to be directed by my hand across the stage.

16th
MOVE

 HUGO BISHOP STOPPED READING.
The silence that came into the room was like the silence that separates the tuning-up of the orchestra and the overture.

Vera Gorringe said:

"That man's going to be a loss to the world."

Bishop nodded, gazing at the open book.

"Yes. What a pity his latest stroke of genius was so uncontrolled. Of course he's utterly unhinged."

"Brilliantly."

"Sometimes that happens. Madness gets into a man's skull and the light blinds before it burns it all away. Shall I read on, Gorry?"

"How long have we?"

Together they looked at the clock. He said:

"Nicole will be here in about an hour. That'll be half an hour to the curtain-up. We've time to follow Pedley's journal to its grave."

Miss Gorringe said nothing. She had put her legs up on the davenport, and now there was a black-and-white striped cushion behind her head. She closed her eyes; her hands were folded loosely on her lap.

The stream of sunlight that slanted down from a wearying sky was now a deeper gold; in its mellow warmth the writing on the pages ran with a spider's unheeding busyness: the tale must be done, come sun or stars.

The woman lay as though sleeping; the man's hand lifted, and turned another page; ninety-three million miles distant, on the other side of the window-glass, the bloodshot eye of the aching sun stared down at the written words:

THE LAST DAY OF MY JOURNAL

And, after that, one more; but it will not be recorded here. My diary is finished, already.

Nicole had the last letter this morning, from Roy Trafford. It said merely that he had seen her at the restaurant with her husband, and had received the note she left. But it does not matter now.

This evening Helen Ledine telephoned me; the girl was out of sorts. She said that Mr. Bishop had called at the Olympus to see her; he told her he had learned the name of Trafford's murderer. I asked her:

"Why did you telephone me?"

"Just to warn you, Harrison."

"Of what?"

"Bishop."

"Why of him?"

She paused for a long time, and then said:

"Harrison, I don't know exactly where your interests lie in this thing. It's occurred to me that the name Bishop has learned might be yours. I don't know; I don't think I care; Roy's dead, isn't he?"

I said nothing.

"So I—felt I should ring you. If I'm wasting my time, that's all right. Forget it. Shall we meet soon?"

"I should like that. I'll telephone you to-morrow, my dear. Thank you for warning me; it is of no consequence, but I appreciate the thought."

When I came away from the instrument that had just cut off my life, I found myself wondering why I had troubled to maintain my pose to Helen; habit, possibly.

Her warning was of the most vital consequence, and only a fool would fail to see it. Here was the justification of my fear, of the unease that cloys my senses when the name of Bishop is spoken. That man might indeed have found me; if he has, he will be here soon.

Shall I run? From what? To where? It is too complicated, and *Othello* has tired me out.

When I returned to the garden, Nicole was reading; I do not know what book; a novel, I think. Within ten minutes the telephone rang again, and Janet came to say that it was for Mrs. Pedley.

Nicole rose and went into the house, and a little while later called from the door of the drawing-room:

"I'm going out for an hour, Harrison."

It was all she could do to force the words; I don't know why.

I looked up from my chair on the lawn, and nodded, and waved a hand to her. Dearly, dearly I should have liked to rise, and hold her just once more, and touch her lifted lips...*One more, and this the last!*

For I feel it would have been.

She went, and a door closed quietly. I had not been possessed of the strength, the courage. Emptied of all good and all evil, all love and all hate, I had not the final flicker of self-will to kiss my heart farewell.

No more than my deserts.

I was summoned to the hideous telephone again, moments later; and it was Mr. Bishop. He asked if he might call: I said he might.

He came, but brought no rosary for me to count in my twilit cell. He brought some pieces he had bargained for at Waring's; and brought, too, all that I had bargained for after Helen's hurried warning...

My dear Bishop: I am sorry that as a host my welcome was less than pardonable; but you came not merely as my guest, but as a host yourself: that of the enemy.

Your chess-pieces are most beautiful, and I am grateful for the sight of their craftsmanship. May you play well with them, and, when checkmate comes, think for a fleeting instant of this greater victory, and of me. For I believe you will not find me a bad loser.

By the way, there is one piece with me still; a red Knight. We mislaid it during our discussion, and I came upon it after you had gone. I will, with every pleasure, return it to you shortly.

I am happy for one thing, that you know me well enough to let me produce my *Othello* to-morrow night. I thank you, a thousand times, for that. If it still lies in my power, you shall witness a production of much accomplishment; my company has worked without stint, and my faith in it is supreme.

Must I record here, finally, my reason for what I did? It is scarcely necessary, for you will have seen it clear enough. I could not reconcile her wanton forsaking of my bright mind for the mere gross caprice offered by a fool's thews. The defence rests.

There is one thing more to say. I have told you all, in this strange journal, except what you set out to discover: the boy Trafford. Or do you already know his present place? You have the clue.

We have sat with him, Nicole and I, on the sunlit lawn, and talked of other things. You played me chess, in the same tranquil place, within some yards of the boy you wished to find. His grave was great, and decked with many lovely hues: aubretia and saxifrage, hyacinth and London Pride.

Little Robert Thorpe told my dear wife of this, when he called at his shop in Tallow Lane. He gave her, as I asked, a packet of aubretia seeds: a few flowers for her lover's grave...

So tell the slut that if she loves the boy, she now knows where to find him. Let her dream upon his handsome face, and see the chill dark earth that dwells in the sockets of his eyes, and watch the worms at their slimy dalliance among his hair! Has she a kiss for him still?

———

Oh, I wish not to have written that; but let it stand; this is the diary of a dying man.

Mr. Bishop, I will see you at the Parthenon perhaps. I trust that you will find much pleasure in the piece.

CHECKMATE

THE LATE SUNLIGHT BURNED in the room, glinting across his nails as the long fingers rippled down the keyboard. On the left hand came the boogie bass-beat with a primitive rhythm that wedded with the lighter notes. It plodded like a gross beast burdened by delicate merchandise.

Vera Gorringe sat at the desk, reading some of the pages that Bishop had spoken aloud from the strange diary of Harrison Pedley. Now and then she glanced up at the Louis XV clock.

They waited for Nicole; in little more than half an hour the curtain would rise on *Othello*.

The music pulsated in the room with its hard, bright theme, and on a couch the Princess Chu Yi-Hsin was widely wakeful, watching the man who worked the great tinkling box.

The cat's eyes gazed; the smoky ears did not move as they attended; the lithe limbs could not relax as the pagan chant of the keys came beating into the sunlit air, beating into the tensed body of the cat in wave on wave of unintelligible, unignorable rhythm. The wild melody reached the soul of the wild creature through the thin shell of civilisation that veneered them both. In the room where stood a telephone, a jungle cat pricked ears to a jungle drum.

The clock chimed the half-hour past six o'clock. The notes, clear and silver and frail, fell across the deeper piano-tones like the ring of shingle down a roaring undertow of surf.

Miss Gorringe looked across at the man who played. His head was a little on one side, his trunk was almost motionless, but the arms moved as if they possessed an independent motivation, and the hands were frenzied as they ravished the instrument with an artist's skill.

They stopped. As the sound ceased, the Siamese remained staring, still bespelled; and then her head lifted, and the wide blue eyes blinked once. The tigress looked up to the higher trees, where the echoes of the drumbeat had fled.

At fifteen minutes past ten o'clock the curtain fell upon the first night of a new *Othello*, a tragedy by

William Shakespeare, at the Parthenon Theatre,
London.

As the company received the applause, a man in
Box D excused himself to the two ladies who were
with him, and left. The quiet closing of the door
was inaudible to them below the warm tide of the
play's reception.

Outside the box were two men; one of them Inspector Frisnay, the other a sergeant. Bishop said:

"Were you out in front at all?"

"No. Was it good?"

"It was very good."

Bishop's face was set, and a little strained; his
eyes brooded for a moment upon his friend's before
he turned along the corridor. "It was memorable,
Freddie. The script is of course immortal; the company is brilliant; the producer was a genius." He
drew a quick, regretful breath. "It's along here, I
think, to the stairs."

As they made their way back-stage the applause
lived on, drumming in the auditorium in waves of
appreciation that was visible, and audible, and tangible. A seal was being set upon a triumph, and as
Bishop reached the tiny office near the dressing-
rooms he cursed softly below his breath, and for
an absurd moment hated his good friend Frisnay.

The moment passed, for it was illogical.

"In here?" Frisnay asked.

"Yes. Mind if I go first?"

"Why?"

"I asked if you minded."

In the distance the applause was dying, voice by voice and hand by hand.

"No. I don't mind."

Bishop knocked at the door. There was no answer. He did not knock again, but turned the handle, and, finding the door unlocked, went in. Pedley was by the little wash-basin in the corner, slumped over its white edge. His hands dropped into the basin, and down them ran the crimson from the severed veins. Bishop said:

"All right, Freddie, I should come in and shut the door."

The two men followed him inside, and the door was closed. Frisnay looked at Pedley, and then turned the key in the lock. He said:

"Expect this?"

Bishop nodded, his eyes attracted to something on the producer's desk.

"Yes. In a way. That's why I asked you to hold off until to-night. Save everyone a lot of trouble all round."

As Frisnay bent over Harrison Pedley and his sergeant stood by, Bishop moved to the desk, and looked down at the little chess-piece that he had left at the house in Hampstead by mistake. The tiny archer bestrode his tiny steed; the bow was flexed inflexibly, with the arrow fixed. The lost red Knight had been returned to him, as Pedley had promised.

He reached down with an idle hand, and picked it up.

"Bishop takes Knight," he murmured, "and that leaves checkmate."